Catherine Stepney

Memoirs of Lady Russell and Lady Herbert

1623-1723

Catherine Stepney

Memoirs of Lady Russell and Lady Herbert
1623-1723

ISBN/EAN: 9783337164751

Printed in Europe, USA, Canada, Australia, Japan

Cover: Foto ©Raphael Reischuk / pixelio.de

More available books at **www.hansebooks.com**

MEMOIRS OF

LADY RUSSELL

AND

LADY HERBERT

1623-1723

COMPILED FROM
ORIGINAL FAMILY DOCUMENTS

BY

LADY STEPNEY

LONDON
ADAM AND CHARLES BLACK
1898

NOTE

THE Memoirs and the Correspondence contained
in this volume were dealt with in works published
from time to time in the earlier half of the century.
It may be considered, however, that they now
come with some freshness ; since the works referred
to have long been out of print, and in this volume
they have been compiled from original family
documents, by Lady Stepney, who lived four
generations ago. The MSS. were left by Lady
Stepney to her son Admiral Manners, by whom
they were bequeathed to Colonel Pollok, her
great-nephew, at whose instance they are now
published.

CONTENTS

LADY RUSSELL

CHAPTER I

AMONG the counsellors and defenders of Charles I. in his adversities, Thomas Wriothesley, Earl of Southampton, was at the same time one of the most faithful and most independent. He was descended from a man of the same name, who was Lord Chancellor under Henry VIII., and was appointed by His Majesty's will one of the sixteen guardians of Edward VI. A younger son, he was suddenly placed in possession of the title and the fortune of his family by the almost simultaneous deaths of his father

1

and his elder brother. His disposition led him to love neither the Court nor his own position. He was more embarrassed than pleased by his elevation, and for some time he coloured and turned away his head when addressed as "My Lord." He was of a melancholy temperament, indolent and proud, with strong passions, reserved and taciturn, much attached to his own ideas and feelings, and ready to make any sacrifice in support of them, but without wish to lead, not sanguine, little excited by success, and leaving his retirement only from duty or necessity.

After passing through college, Lord Southampton spent some time on the Continent, where he met the lady who became his first wife. On his return to his native country, he lived in private, taking little part in politics. When, however, the struggle between Charles I. and the Long

Parliament began, he took his place in the House of Lords, where he showed himself disposed to support the demands of the people, rather than the arbitrary acts and pretensions of the Crown and its Ministers. A true patriot, he wished the laws and customs of the nation to be respected, and the Parliament to have a part in the government of the country. Moderate in his religious views, he desired greater toleration and charity towards Dissenters. Although he did not regard freedom of opinion as a right, tyranny in affairs of conscience was repugnant to him. At the beginning of the Long Parliament, he frequently voted against the Crown, against the Bishops, and for the reform of abuses, and the restraint of despotism, both religious and political. He seldom appeared at Court, was looked upon as attached to the party in opposition to the Crown, and among those who surrounded

the King was regarded as being, like his
friend and relation the Earl of Essex, discontented and moody; but when he saw
the violence and injustice with which the
proceedings of Parliament were conducted,
the laws violated, and the Monarchy en-
dangered by popular tumults under the
leading of ambitious and unscrupulous men,
he immediately took his place, not from
inclination, but from a feeling of duty, among
the defenders and servants of the King.
Holding himself aloof from all party combina-
tions, without any definite plan, troubling
himself little with the reform of the Constitution, or with abstract theories of government,
he opposed the prevalent injustice, inequality,
disorder, and violence, without concerning
himself with the schemes of those who took
part in them. The proceedings of Parliament
against Lord Strafford appeared to him
arbitrary, the penalty excessive; and he

defended him whom he had previously opposed. The Houses had voted that it was improper for members to take office under the Crown: he accepted, though unwillingly, that of Privy Councillor, and afterwards that of Lord of the Bed-chamber. He steadily supported the King against the violence of the popular party, as he had previously supported the claims of the people against the oppression of the Court. The Civil War broke out. He detested it, and looked for no good result, whichever side prevailed; but immediately joined the royal army, was present at the battle of Edgehill, and followed the Court to Oxford, though every day more and more dissatisfied with its conduct. He retained all his independence and his proud susceptibility.

On one occasion in the Council he expressed himself in strong language respecting the arrogant pretensions over the English

nobility put forward by Prince Rupert. The
Prince, to whom an exaggerated report had
been made of what had passed, asked him
if it were true. The Earl acknowledged
what he had said, repeating the exact words.
Rupert persisted in finding them offensive,
and caused him to be informed that he
expected to receive satisfaction for them, and
to meet him on horseback sword in hand.
They met next morning.

"What arms do you choose?" said the
Prince.

"I have no suitable horse here," said the
Earl. "I could not obtain one immediately.
Moreover, I am too small and too weak to
compete with Your Highness in this manner.
I must beg you to excuse me, and to allow
me to choose arms of which I can make use.
I will fight on foot, and with pistols."

Rupert agreed without hesitation. The
seconds were appointed, and the meeting was

fixed for the next day; but the affair had become public; the Lords of the Council interfered, caused the gates of the town to be closed, summoned the seconds, and reconciled the Earl and the Prince.

When the war had ended, and the King was in the hands of the Parliament, Lord Southampton made every possible effort for his deliverance, and sought diligently for the means of seeing and of assisting him. When all had failed, and the trial, condemnation, and execution of Charles left nothing to attempt or to hope, he did not consider himself released from his duty towards his royal master. On the 8th of February 1649, the day when the remains of Charles I. were buried at Windsor, Lord Southampton was one of five who accompanied to the tomb the Prince whom he had been unable either to enlighten or to save. Snow was falling thickly, and the black velvet pall which covered

the coffin was completely whitened; which
the faithful servants of the King afterwards
delighted to recall, as a symbol of innocence.

Royalty having been abolished, Lord
Southampton returned to his retirement at
Titchfield, and throughout the duration of
the Republic and the Protectorate of Cromwell he employed himself with his family,
and in the improvement of his estate, taking
no part in public affairs, remaining always
faithful to the proscribed Charles II., send-
ing him useful intelligence, and frequent
and liberal supplies of money, but joining
neither in the attempted insurrections of the
Royalists nor in the movements of discontented Republicans. His good sense, his
jealous patriotism, and his natural indolence
combined to keep him in this honourable
inactivity. He was one day informed that
Cromwell, who was on a visit in Hampshire,
on the occasion of the marriage of his son

Richard, had shown some intention of surprising him by a visit. Lord Southampton immediately left his house, and did not return until Cromwell had quitted the county.

On the Restoration, Lord Southampton, notwithstanding his inactivity during the interregnum, was among the · first of the nobles and former councillors of Charles I. whom Royalist feeling called to office. Hyde, who then possessed the King's confidence, was his particular friend. He was made Lord Treasurer when Hyde became Chancellor and Earl of Clarendon; and for seven years he performed the duties of the office with a vigilance, integrity, and disinterestedness not always agreeable to the monarch and his profligate Court. The two friends, united in principle though different in character, controlled with difficulty a King without virtue or feeling, a corrupt and intriguing Court, a victorious but discontented

Party, and a people austere, humiliated, and wrathful. Clarendon, ambitious, laborious, enthusiastic for his Church, his cause, his power, and his rank, struggled violently against his enemies, old and new, and against the decline of his influence with his former pupil, now become his Sovereign. Southampton, less energetic, fond of leisure and repose, with greater liberality of mind, tormented, moreover, by gout and stone,[1] conscientiously performed the duties of his office. He made ineffectual efforts towards having the resources of the Crown administered in order and good faith, and, frequently desponding, disgusted and ill, made known, to the great chagrin of Clarendon, his wish to quit an office which he filled without pleasure and without success.

Charles, as clear - sighted as he was

[1] Burnet says he bore his sufferings " with astonishing patience, the firmness of a great man, and the submission of a good Christian."

corrupt, soon perceived that Lord Southampton was indifferent to power, and wished
to take advantage of this feeling in order to
get rid quietly of an independent and unwel-
come councillor ; but Clarendon employed
all the influence he still retained to keep his
friend in office ; and Lord Southampton,
Treasurer till his death, quitted life and
public business together, without yielding,
like the Chancellor, to the unjust hatred of
the people, or to the ungrateful severity of
the King.

Lord Southampton had married Rachel
de Ruvigny, a member of one of those
noble French families who in the sixteenth
century, without any view to personal
interest, or any thought of increase in power
or wealth, from the mere dictates of faith
and conscience, embraced the cause of the
Reformation, which was at all times feeble
in France, and from its infancy subject to

persecution. At the time of their marriage the Edict of Nantes was still in force. Richelieu, although he had destroyed the political power of the Protestants, did not interfere with their religious rights, and did not hesitate to employ in various public offices those who showed themselves devoted to the interests of the Crown and to himself. Mazarin followed Richelieu's example. He was equally prudent as to the religious liberty of Protestants, but 'more cautious as to their employment in affairs of state. Though unmolested and enjoying the liberty allowed by the Edict, the Protestants, in a minority and subjection, daily lost in the strength that is derived from real activity, which alone gives importance in public opinion and secures freedom. Their places of worship were still open ; they were not driven from their country ; but they were restricted to private life, isolated, and, as it were, foreigners. The Marquess de Ruvigny, brother of Lady Southampton, possessed great ability and courage, and was one of the most important and intelligent among the Protestants of that period. During the disturbances of the Fronde, he gave Anne of Austria and Mazarin proofs of fidelity, constant, active, and important. When the Fronde was suppressed, Mazarin, wishing to reward Ruvigny, caused him to be appointed Deputy-General of the National Synod of the French Reformed Churches, a double and intermediary office, which made him the *chargé d'affaires* of the King towards the Protestants and of the Protestants towards the King. Ruvigny performed this double duty for nearly thirty years, with a well-governed zeal, often disagreeable, and even suspected by both parties, but equally faithful to the King and to the Church, and giving himself little disquiet as to either

being pleased, provided he managed to pre-
serve peace between them and to maintain
their respective rights. This, however, did
not afford a sufficient object in life. Wishing
to have a pursuit, he attempted to obtain
employment, either in the army or in diplomacy abroad; but was given to understand
that he would find everything of that kind
unattainable unless he changed his religion.
The King and the Church made use of him
with the Protestants, he being the only person
capable of treating with them; but all other
openings were closed to him. After the
death of Mazarin, and the restoration of the
Stewarts, Ruvigny's many connections in
England, his intimate relations with the
Southampton and Bedford families, and
with others of importance both in the Court
Party and in the Opposition, obtained for
him without any effort on his part what he
had previously sought in vain. He was

repeatedly employed in the most confidential negotiations between the courts of Paris and London, endeavouring sometimes to arrange the secret agreements of the two Kings, sometimes to secure the secret influence of Louis XIV. over the most active leaders of the Opposition in Parliament. Louis had a sincere esteem for him, and Charles showed him special favour. Writing to his sister the Duchess of Orleans, he said that France had never shown itself so friendly as since he had resided in London. Loving his country, a devoted Royalist, and a sincere Protestant, Ruvigny made great endeavours to serve at the same time his King, his country, and his faith, yet without deceiving himself as to the probability of this difficult conciliation being long maintained. The Edict of Nantes still stood, but like a deserted and ruined building which needs only the blow of a hammer to bring it down. Under the pressure of

a general feeling among the Catholics of
France, and the urgent desires of the clergy,
—wishing, also, to carry out the false and
fatal idea that power has rights over conscience and that the unity of the State requires
unity of faith,—Louis XIV., with a want of
fidelity which he would not have allowed
himself towards strangers, set at naught—
sometimes secretly, sometimes publicly—the
royal promises and the legal guarantees
which had been given by his ancestors to
a part of his subjects. The Marquess de
Ruvigny, whilst serving the King, was not
blind to the end towards which His Majesty
was proceeding. Resolved, when the final
issue approached, to sacrifice everything
rather than his faith, he had secured letters
of naturalisation in England for himself and
his children. In January 1680, he wrote to
his niece, Lady Russell :

" I send you my letters of naturalisation,

which will be better in your hands than in mine. I would beg you and your sister to take care of them for me. They may be useful, since there is nothing more uncertain than the course of events."

Affairs did not remain uncertain long. Five years afterwards the Edict of Nantes was formally revoked; and Ruvigny obtained with great difficulty, as the reward of his services, and from the personal favour of Louis XIV., the privilege of becoming with his family exiled from his country without flight—he was the only nobleman to whom this favour was granted. Some years afterwards, in 1711, the King bestowed upon the Abbé de Polignac the confiscated property of his son, Henry de Ruvigny, who had entered the service of William III. and had been made Lord Galway.

The revocation of the Edict of Nantes, in addition to its general effects upon the population and the wealth of the country, cost France the services of three excellent officers : Marshal Schomberg in the army, Admiral Duquesne in the navy, and the Marquess de Ruvigny in diplomacy.

CHAPTER II

LADY SOUTHAMPTON had five children, only two of whom survived her. The younger of them, born in 1636, was named Rachel, after her mother. Descended from two noble families, educated in habits of piety and virtue, she received from the events of her youth those strong moral impressions which elevate minds that are not oppressed by them. She early learned to feel for the misfortunes of others, and to bear domestic trials with patience. When she was an infant she had lost her mother. Lord Southampton married again;[1] but he never

---

[1] Lord Southampton was married three times. His second wife, the daughter of Sir Francis Leigh, afterwards Earl of Chichester, had four daughters, one of whom survived her parents, and was

ceased to entertain the most tender affection
for the two daughters whom his first
wife had left him, nor did Rachel respect or love her father the less.   She
saw him devote himself without the least
illusion or servility of mind to that political
cause which, all things considered, he
believed to have most justice on its side,
and remain at the same time both patriot
and Royalist.   The principles of integrity,
liberality, and piety, which were character-
istics of his own mind, were instilled by
precept and example into the minds of his
daughters.   His religion was not merely a
system of forms and ceremonies.   As is
evident from Burnet's testimony already

married to the last Earl of Northumberland of the Percy family,
and after his death to Mr. (afterwards Lord) Montagu. She is
often mentioned in Lady Russell's letters as Countess of Northumberland, and as Lady Montagu. The Earl's third wife was
Frances, daughter of the Duke of Somerset, and widow of Viscount
Molineux. She long survived Lord Southampton, and afterwards
married Mr. D'Arcy, who also is mentioned in Lady Russell's
letters.

quoted, it was a communion of his soul
with his heavenly Father, through the
Saviour. At the period when she passed
from childhood to youth, she lived in the
country, far from the world, familiarised
with those habits of quiet dignity, simplicity,
polite manners, and general benevolence
which do honour to a Christian aristocracy.
We have not much information respecting
her education; but there is no reason to
suppose that it was inferior to that of other
ladies in her rank of life. Her letters show
a well-trained mind; and her having been
the only governess of her two daughters,
afterwards the Duchesses of Devonshire
and Rutland, would indicate that her own
education had not been neglected. Among
her early instructors may be reckoned
Dr. Fitzwilliam, who was for many years
chaplain to her father, and afterwards to
the Duke of York, and took an almost

parental interest in her, as is evident from the letters on both sides which have been preserved.

In 1653, at the age of seventeen, she was handsome, pious, and cheerful, without highly-wrought imaginations, disposed to enjoy life quietly, receiving good things as favours, and evils as lessons, from God. A marriage with Lord Vaughan, the elder son of Lord Carbery, was concluded by an arrangement between their respective parents, while yet they were scarce acquainted with one another. It was one of those marriages in which, as she afterwards said when speaking of that of one of her friends, "it is acceptance rather than choosing on either side." She went to live at the residence of her father-in-law, Golden Grove, in Wales, and fulfilled all the duties of her new situation without effort, and without display, inspiring those about her with a

lively affection, but producing no other
impression than that of constant virtue, an
agreeable temper, and especially of such
perfect amiability that it was spoken of to
herself as a peculiar merit, her correspondent,
after a high-flown compliment, concluding:
" Present your noble husband with my most
affectionate service, and I shall in my prayers
present you both to God, begging of Him
daily increase of your piety to Him, and of
your love to each other." [1]

Little is known of the character of Lord
Vaughan; but it may be presumed that an
affectionate father, as Lord Southampton
evidently was, would not arrange an alliance
for his daughter with one who was likely to
endanger her happiness. That her conduct
was such as to obtain the approbation of her

[1] Lord Carbery was the protector of Jeremy Taylor, whose
Holy Living and Dying was dedicated to him; another of
Taylor's works, *Golden Grove*, is named after Lord Carbery's
estate.

husband's family is shown by her having continued on friendly terms with them all her life, and by her having exerted her influence in their favour many years after his death.

Fourteen years thus passed with Lady Vaughan, calmly and virtuously happy. From an unfinished paper found after her death, it would appear that this time of her life was characterised by greater intercourse and conformity with the world than she allowed herself at any other period. She regrets her coldness and formality in religious duties, and her too great liking for plays and other diversions. This, however, probably arose, not from her having indulged in frivolous pursuits to excess, but from her having attained a more lively sense of the importance of religion during her residence with her elder sister in her first widowhood, and from habits of reflection formed during her seclusion after Lord Russell's death.

In 1665 she bore a child, which died almost immediately. In 1667 she was a widow. No details of the death of her husband are recorded; but the plague raged in London in 1665-66, extending to many places in the country; and probably he was one of its victims. She then lived with her sister, Lady Elizabeth Noel,[1] at Titchfield, the house of her father, in which she had passed her childhood. Lord Southampton died in 1667, leaving Titchfield to Lady Elizabeth Noel, and Stratton, also in Hampshire, to Lady Vaughan. His property in London was divided between the two sisters, his youngest daughter being provided for by her mother's fortune.

About the time of Lord Southampton's death a young man, three years the junior of Lady Vaughan, the second surviving son

[1] For more than a century after her death, which occurred about 1679 or 1680, traditions of the piety and the charity of Lady Elizabeth Noel were preserved among the cottagers at Titchfield.

of the Earl of Bedford,[1] began to take part in
public life, but not as yet very prominently.
After travelling on the Continent for three
years, he had returned to England a short
time before the Restoration, and had been
elected a member of the House of Commons
which recalled Charles II. Few traces of
his life and character at this period remain.
A note to him from his tutor, Mr. Thornton,
shows that religion had not been neglected

---

[1] The family of the Russells first appears in public life in the
reign of Henry VII. In the year 1506 the King and Queen of
Castile left the Low Countries for Spain. Their fleet was dispersed in
the Channel by a violent storm, and the ship in which they were with
difficulty ran into Weymouth. As soon as they were landed, Sir
Thomas Trenchard, the High Sheriff of the county, paid his respects
and invited them to his house at Wolveton. As he was not
acquainted with the Spanish language, he applied to Mr. Russell,
who lived at a short distance, to come and interpret for them.
Henry VII. having sent the Earl of Arundel to invite Philip to
Windsor, the latter, on leaving, asked Sir Thomas if he could do
anything for him with the King. Sir Thomas answered that he
was not himself in want of anything, but that if Philip could do
anything for Mr. Russell, he should take it as done to himself.
Philip, accordingly, took Mr. Russell with him, and warmly
recommended him to the King. Henry VII. created him Lord
Russell, and named him one of his executors; and he was afterwards made Earl of Bedford by Edward VI.

in his upbringing, and one from him to
Mr. Thornton, after a severe illness, indicates
that it had not been altogether without
effect. He says :

" My prayers to God are to give me, together with my health, grace to employ it in
His service, and to make good use of this
visitation by the serious application of it."

His religious impressions do not, however, appear to have been very decided
until later. The manners of the times, the
example of the Court, the heat of youth,
and perhaps also his natural temper, led him
into some irregularities of conduct; and he
was engaged in more than one duel. This
did not long continue.[1] His conduct became

---

[1] Bishop Burnet says of him : " He was a man of great candour,
and of a general reputation ; universally beloved and trusted ; of a
generous, obliging temper. He gave proof of undaunted courage,
and of an unshaken firmness. He quickly got out of some disorders
into which the Court had drawn him, and ever after that his life was
unblemished in all respects. He had from his first education an
inclination to favour the Nonconformists, and wished the laws

more in accord with the pious instructions
he had received, and it is not improbable
that Lady Vaughan exercised an unconscious
influence in the correction of the irregularities in the life of the young man to whom
she was afterwards united. Of all human
motives, there is none which has so much
power as a virtuous attachment. There is
no account of their early acquaintance. We
only know, by a letter of Lady Percy, Lady
Vaughan's half-sister, that he was attached to
the handsome widow in 1667. She says:

" For his concern, I can say nothing more
than that he professes a great desire, which
I do not at all doubt he, and everybody else
has, to gain one who is so desirable in all
respects."

could have been made more easy to them, or they more pliant to
the law. He was a slow man, and of little discourse ; but he had
a true judgment. When he considered things at his own leisure,
his understanding was not defective ; but his virtues were so
eminent that they would more than have balanced real defects, if
any had been found."

Lady Vaughan was without children, and was a great heiress. William Russell, a younger son, had neither fortune nor a title to offer. He was the more timid and reserved on that account. But there was too much sympathy in their natural dispositions for worldly considerations and doubts to keep them long apart. They were married about the end of the year 1669; but, according to the usual custom in England at that time, Lady Vaughan retained her title till 1678, when, the elder brother of Mr. Russell having died, he became heir to his father, and assumed the title of Lord Russell.

CHAPTER III

ONE of the most charming sights in the world is a married pair united by a true affection based on congeniality of sentiment and principle. Passion, the open and generous expression of the feelings and inmost capacities of the soul, has such attraction for us, that we take pleasure in regarding its manifestation, even when accompanied with disorder, mistakes, troubles, and sorrows; but passion in harmony with principle, and filling the heart with a flood of happiness, without overclouding the mind or interrupting its peace, is the most active emotion of our being, and possesses the greatest interest to those who behold it. The union of

Rachel Wriothesley and William Russell was of this rare character. Hitherto she had been tranquil, simple, calmly pursuing the ordinary paths of life. Now passionate affection and the highest earthly happiness filled her heart. She gave herself up to their influence, and manifested them without reserve : she ardently loved her husband, and was entirely happy. They were seldom separated, and only for short periods, during the fourteen years of their married life. Consequently, but few of their letters remain. Those which we have present, on both sides, a pleasing picture of conjugal confidence and domestic happiness. It is evident that they found their chief pleasure in the faithful discharge of their duties to each other, and in promoting the welfare and the happiness of those around them.

"If I were more fortunate," she writes, three years after their marriage, "in my expression, I could do myself more right when I would own to my dearest Mr. Russell what real and perfect happiness I enjoy, from that kindness he allows me every day to receive new marks of, such as, in spite of the knowledge I have of my own wants, will not suffer me to mistrust I want his love, though I do merit, to so desirable a blessing ; but, my best life, you that know so well how to love and to oblige, make my felicity entire, by believing my heart possessed with all the gratitude, honour, and passionate affection to your person, any creature is capable of, or can be obliged to."

Three years later she says :

" It is an inexpressible joy to consider, I shall see the person in the world I most and only long to be with, before another week is past. I should condemn my sense of this expected happiness as weak and pitiful if I could tell it you. No, my best life : I can say little, but think all you can, and you cannot think too much; my heart makes it all good. I perfectly know my infinite obligations to Mr. Russell; and it is the delight of her life, who is as much yours as you desire she should be."

Again, five years afterwards:

"My dearest heart, flesh and blood cannot have a truer and greater sense of their own happiness than your poor but honest wife has. I am glad you find Stratton so sweet; may you live to do so one fifty years more; and if God pleases, I shall be glad I may keep your company most of those years, unless you wish for other at any time; then I think I could willingly leave all in the world, knowing you would take care of our brats; they are both well, and your great one's letter she hopes came to you."

Again: "These are pleasing moments, in absence, my dearest blessing, either to read something from you, or to be writing something to you; yet I never do it but I am touched with a sensible regret that I cannot pour out in words what my heart is so big with, which is much more just to your dear self (in a passionate return of love and gratitude) than I can tell you; but it is not my talent, and so I hope not a necessary signification of the truth of it : at least not thought so by you."

A year later : " To see anybody preparing, and taking their way to see what I long to do a thousand times more than they, makes me not endure to suffer their going, without saying something to my best life; though it is a kind of anticipating my joy when we shall meet, to allow myself so much, before the time; but I confess I feel a great deal, that, though I left London with great reluctance (as it is easy to persuade men a woman does), yet that I am not like to leave

Stratton with greater. . . . I would fain be telling my heart more things—anything, to be in a kind of talk with him ; but, I believe, Spencer stays for my despatch ; he was willing to go early ; but this was to be the delight of this morning and the support of the day. It is performed in bed, thy pillow at my back ; where thy dear head shall lie, I hope, to-morrow night, and many more, I trust in His mercy, notwithstanding all our enemies or ill-wishers. Love and be willing to be loved by R. Russell."

Lady Russell did not express her love to her husband merely in writing. She showed it actively, in the smallest, as well as in the greatest, things : taking interest in all his occupations, in all his tastes ; living with him in the world when he would mix with the world, in the country when he preferred the country ; caring for his amusements, as well as for his happiness.

When they were separated — the one at
Stratton, the other in London—she kept
herself informed on political and fashionable
affairs, the affairs of their friends, and the
incidents of society, and communicated them
to him speedily, without study of expression,
or attempt to show herself off, but as one
simply desirous of collecting all that could
interest or divert him.   In May 1672 she
writes :

"I am very sure my dearest Mr. Russell
meant to oblige me extremely when he
enjoined me to scribble to him by the post,
as knowing he could not do a kinder thing
than to let me see he designed not to think
me impertinent in it; though we parted but
this morning, which I might reasonably have
doubted to have been when I have passed
all this long day and learned nothing new
can entertain you and your good company.
. All I see either are or appear duller to me

than when you are here; and I do not find the town is enlivened by the victory we have obtained. There is no more talked of than you heard last night, nor nothing printed, because there is no letters come yet; Tom Howard, Lord Howard's son, is expected every hour with them. Many whisper the French behaved themselves not like firm friends. The Duke of York's marriage is broke off. That, or other causes, makes him look less in good humour than ordinary. They say she is offered the King of Spain; and our Prince shall have D'Elbœuf. Mrs. Ogle is to marry Craven Howard, Tom Howard's son; and Tom Wharton has another mistress in chase, my Lady Rochester's grandchild; but he is so unfortunate before the end, that it is mistrusted he may miss her, though the grandmother is his great friend. Young Arundel, my Lord Arundel of Trerice his son, is extremely

in love, and went down where she is, and
watched her coming abroad to take the air,
rode up to her coach. Mr. Wharton was on
horse by the roadside. Arundel thrust him
away, and, looking into the coach, told her
no man durst say he valued her at the rate
he did. Mr. Wharton, like a good Christian,
turned the other cheek; for he took no
notice of it; but the other, having no opportunity to see or speak to her, was thus
forced to return; but Wharton is admitted
to the house."

Besides the love for her husband, another affection animated Lady Russell and
strengthened her beforehand for her day of
trial. She was a Christian, not in name
only, but also in mind and heart, with an
entire belief in Christian truth, submissive
to Christian precepts, without sectarianism,
without taste for disputation, moved by an
intelligent and exalted charity towards those

who did not think exactly as she thought. Her letters after the blow had fallen show in what uncommon harmony Christian feeling and human affection were united in her. She had the power of faith in her soul in the midst of her happiness, and, while she was still in the enjoyment of it, prepared herself with humility to accept from the hand of God the strokes, or rather the stroke, of which she seems to have had some presentiment. In 1680 she wrote:

"Absent or present, my dearest life is equally obliging, and ever the earthly delight of my soul; it is my great care (or ought to be) so to moderate my sense of happiness here, that when the appointed time comes of my leaving it, or its leaving me, I may not be unwilling to forsake the one, or be in some measure prepared and fit to bear the trial of the other. What have I to ask but a continuance (if God see fit) of these present

enjoyments? If not, a submission without
murmur to His most wise dispensations and
unerring providence, having a thankful heart
for the years I have been so perfectly
contented in; He knows best when we have
had enough here; what I most earnestly beg
from His mercy is, that we both live so as,
whichever goes first, the other may not
sorrow as for one of whom they have no
hope. Then let us cheerfully expect to be
together to a good old age; if not, let us not
doubt but He will support us under what
trial He will inflict upon us. These are
necessary meditations sometimes, that we
may not be surprised above our strength
by a sudden accident, being unprepared.
Excuse me, if I dwell too long upon it; it is
from my opinion that if we can be prepared
for all conditions, we can with the greater
tranquillity enjoy the present, which I hope
will be long; though when we change, it will

be for the better, I trust, through the merits of Christ. Let us daily pray that it may be so, and then admit of no fears : death is the extremest evil against nature, it is true; let us overcome the immoderate fear of it, either to our friend or self, and then what light hearts we may live with."

Ten years elapsed since Lady Russell in London had written these words to her husband at Stratton. Lord Russell was in London, and his wife at Stratton, when, on September 25, 1682, she wrote :

"I know nothing new since you went; but I know as certainly as I live, that I have been for twelve years as passionate a lover as ever woman was, and hope to be so one twelve years more; happy still and entirely yours,   R. RUSSELL."

Lady Russell's attachments were not hastily formed ; but they were lasting. She was susceptible of conjugal and maternal affection in no ordinary degree. Almost every letter after the birth of her children contains some reference to them. She was also a kind and considerate mistress, not merely satisfying herself with ordering that medical advice should be provided for a sick servant; but herself making inquiry of the physician as to the state of his patient, and reporting the result to her husband.

Scarcely ten months had passed since Lady Russell wrote the letter, so full of affection, happiness, and trust, from which the last extract was taken, when the lightning fell in the midst of a sky so calm and peaceful. Lord Russell was a prisoner in the Tower, and was charged with high treason at the bar of the Old Bailey Sessions. He had sat in the House of Commons for several years, without taking much part, or much interest, in the debates. He was young, and led into other courses by the ardour of youth. He was a man, not of showy talents, but of high-toned principle and unshrinking firmness; and "in all probability he would have continued through life an inactive representative had not extraordinary events called forth the native energy of his character, never afterwards to sleep, but on the scaffold."[1]

[1] *Memoir of William, Lord Russell,* by Lord John Russell.

CHAPTER IV

THE hopes which had been raised in England by the Restoration were slowly dissipated. Recollections of the Commonwealth and the Protectorate, and the reaction against the maxims, the acts, and the agents of those times, filled all minds. Charles II. and his Court, with licentious self-indulgence, took advantage of these strong feelings, till their pretensions, their faults, their vices, excited fresh disputes and roused men's passions anew. A life insulting to the moral as well as to the political feelings of the people had shaken their love for the Sovereign not a little. But "an attachment to foreign interests, and the profession of an

.odious religion, had excited the strongest aversion to the presumptive successor to the Throne."[1] The old Royalists, the men who had fought for Charles I. and resisted Cromwell, had disappeared. New men, and, under their leading, new parties, appeared on the scene: the Party of the Crown and the Party of the Country, afterwards the Tories and the Whigs, descendants of the Cavaliers and Roundheads, but greatly transformed. Parliament had become the arena and the indispensable instrument of politics. The Royalist Long Parliament carried on, while they detested, the work of the Revolutionary Long Parliament. The restored Monarchy triumphed by means of the same arms which had struck it down. The King governed the country by Parliament, and the Parliament, by its own leaders, became the adviser of the Crown.

[1] *Memoir of William, Lord Russell.*

It was not till some little time after Russell's marriage to Lady Vaughan that he began to take a prominent position in the Country Party. His first speech was in 1674. With generous feelings, an elevated but not very comprehensive mind, and little foresight, of a character more obstinate than strong, and disposed to allow himself to be easily led, or governed, or deceived, in the course to which his inclination disposed him, he soon became one of the most fervent opponents of the Court, and the ornament, if not the chief leader, of the Country Party. The principles which he adopted and the measures which he brought forward or supported would necessarily bring on him the resentment of those whose corruption he resisted. Always ready to risk danger in behalf of his cause, he undertook the defence in the House of Commons, and often the initiative, of the strongest measures of the Opposition—among others, the Bill by which it was proposed to exclude the Duke of York from the succession, as being a Papist. He had the merit with his Party and in the nation of almost always sharing their prejudices, their passions, their mistakes; agreeing with them in judgment and in feeling, superior to them all by his virtues. Thus he soon became the man who was most popular and most honoured in the Kingdom, and such was the mutual agreement and sympathy between him and the National Party that nothing occurred to enlighten Lord Russell as to his failings, or those of his friends—for the only warnings of them came from his opponents, and such warnings are never much regarded.

Lady Russell, whilst she sympathised with her husband's principles, both political and religious, and honoured him for his steadfast adherence to them, was not blind to the danger he incurred ; and, from doubts as to the propriety of some of the measures he proposed, or disquieted as to their probable consequence, sometimes gave him cautions on the subject with a frankness equally tender and firm. In 1681 she concludes a letter thus :

" One remembrance more, my best life. Be wise as a serpent, harmless as a dove. So farewell for this time."

On another occasion she says :

" Look to your pockets ; a printed paper says you will have fine papers put into them, and then witnesses to swear."

Like himself, she was anxiously and patriotically occupied with the future of her country ; but her judgment was more untrammelled, less prejudiced, more far-sighted. As early as March 1678, when Lord Russell was about to support a measure of bitter opposition in the House of Commons, he received a note from her during the sitting :

" My sister, being here, tells me she overheard you tell her Lord last night, that you would take notice of the business (you know what I mean) in the House ; this alarms me, and I do earnestly beg of you to tell me truly if you have or mean to do it ; if you do, I am most assured you will repent it. I beg once more to know the truth. It is more pain to be in doubt, and to your sister too ; and if I have any interest, I use it to beg your silence in this case, at least to-day.

" R. RUSSELL."

It is not necessary to read this letter a second time in order to be convinced that this was not the first occasion on which Lady Russell had used similar language. Her urgent request that he would tell her the truth implies a mild complaint that he had often concealed it from her, and a lively solicitude on account of what she could not be sure to prevent. Lord Russell was no doubt struck with the step she had taken; for he carefully preserved the note, marking on it the time and the place where it was received. It is, however, probable that he did not follow her advice, either then or on other similar occasions.

The time arrived when the King, though little inclined to a hazardous line of policy, and the Parliament, though monarchical and loyal, came to an open rupture. The National Party required Charles II. to disinherit his brother, and with his own hands to divert the succession from the direct line. Charles required the National Party, at all risks, to submit to a Prince who evidently desired to destroy the religion and the constitution of the country. Thus pushed to extremes, each formed a resolution: the King to attempt tyranny; the National Party, insurrection. At the critical moment, in 1681, when the last Parliament of Charles II. was dissolved, two men, Lord Shaftesbury and Lord Russell, were the leaders of the struggle. Shaftesbury was already old, ambitious, indefatigable, and corrupt, practised from childhood in seeking and finding his fortune in intrigues and plots. His was a bold and flexible mind, sagacious and fertile, having great influence over men : he was equally able to serve or to injure, to please or to perplex, but attached by pride and foresight to the Protestant and National Party, which appeared to him the stronger, and certain ultimately to prevail. He was fully resolved amid any circumstances to save himself : to reap the fruit of his intrigues, or to renew them. Lord Russell was still young, sincere, ardent, inexperienced, firm in mind and heart, full of faith and honour, conscientious even in conspiring, ready to sacrifice his life in the cause, but incapable of indifference to success or of taking flight. Between these two men, engaged with such different feelings in the same enterprise, it was easy to foresee which would be the instrument in case of success, or the victim in case of failure.

The conspirators met from time to time, doubtful of each other and not revealing to each other the full extent of their projects. Lord Russell, with Algernon Sidney, was willing to organise a resistance to arbitrary power, and to exclude the Duke of York from the Throne, probably accepting in the depths of his soul, without avowing it even to himself, the consequences of such a revolution. Lord Shaftesbury saw clearly into his design, and was prepared at all costs for the dethronement of the King and the appointment of a successor other than the direct heir. There were others who desired to have a Republican Government, and, in pursuit of their dream, were prepared for the deaths of the King and the Duke. There were among them also traitors, either bought by the Court or ready to give up the secret and sacrifice their associates in order to save themselves. One day, when they were assembled, Lord Russell saw enter, with Colonel Sidney and Hampden, Lord Howard of Escrick, a man whom he distrusted, who was afterwards one of the chief witnesses against him. He expressed to his friend Lord Essex his wish to withdraw; but Lord Essex detained him, thinking better of Lord Howard, and little suspecting that he would be the instrument of the ruin of them both.

Some days later, Lord Mordaunt, an ardent Royalist and far from being a conspirator, although a friend of Lord Shaftesbury, was with the Duchess of Portsmouth, the King's mistress, with whom he had

formed a secret and close intimacy, in the
hope of advancing his fortune. Suddenly
the King's arrival was announced to the
Duchess: His Majesty was on the stairs.
The Duchess hastily concealed Lord Mordaunt in an adjoining room. Curiosity led
him to look through the keyhole. Lord
Howard had come, and was conversing with
the King, but in a voice so low that it could
not be overheard. Released by the Duchess
as soon as she herself was free, Mordaunt
hastened out, took a coach, and went forth-
with to Lord Shaftesbury, whom he informed
of what he had witnessed.

"Are you quite certain?" asked the Earl,
regarding him steadfastly.

"Perfectly sure," said Mordaunt.

"Well, my Lord, you are an honourable
young man: you would not deceive me. If
that is true, I must be off to-night."

Lord Shaftesbury did leave his house that

night, and concealed himself elsewhere in London, — the order for his arrest was issued the following day,—and some days afterwards he embarked at Harwich and took refuge in Holland, hoping to find an asylum there and an avenger in the Prince of Orange. As Chancellor, he had vehemently supported the war against Holland, and more than once had said, "Carthage must be destroyed." On arriving at Amsterdam, he applied to the Burgomaster for permission to reside there. "Carthage, not yet destroyed, willingly receives the Earl of Shaftesbury within her walls," the Burgomaster answered.

At the same time that the order was given for the arrest of Lord Shaftesbury, a similar order had been issued for that of Lord Russell, and that he should be brought before the Council. The messenger who bore the order presented himself at the chief entrance of the house ; but that at the back was left free, probably by design. Lord Russell might have escaped ; but he would not, saying that his flight would be a confession, and that he had done nothing which should make him fear the justice of his country. Nevertheless, he sent Lady Russell hastily to consult his chief friends, who, understanding that his accuser was a man named Rumsey, whom Lord Russell had never trusted—whose testimony, there-fore, he did not fear—agreed that he ought not to fly.

He appeared before the King and Council. The King told him that he was not suspected of any design against him personally, but that there were strong proofs of his intentions against the Government. After a long examination, he was sent to the Tower. On entering, he said to his valet, Taunton, that there was a determination against him, and that they would take his life. On Taunton's expressing a hope that his enemies would not succeed, "They will take it," repeated Lord Russell: "the devil is unchained."

"From the moment of his arrest," says Burnet, "he looked upon himself as a dying man, and turned his thoughts wholly to another world. He read much in the Scriptures, particularly in the Psalms. But, whilst he behaved with the serenity of a man prepared for death, his friends exhibited an honourable anxiety to save his life. Lord Essex would not leave his house, lest his absconding might incline a jury to give more credit to the evidence against Lord Russell. The Duke of Monmouth offered to come in, and share fortunes with him, if he could do him any service. But he answered, 'it would be of no advantage to him to have his friends die with him.'"

We need not repeat the details of the trial. Our purpose is merely to describe the domestic life of Lord and Lady Russell, their feelings towards each other, under trials, as well as in happier times. As soon as her husband was arrested, Lady Russell rose equal to the emergency, and devoted herself to the measures for his assistance with an ardour and intelligence which called forth the admiration of all who observed it. During the fortnight which elapsed between his arrest and the sentence, she went, came, wrote, without ceasing, collected intelligence, raised the courage of alarmed friends, excited the interest of persons who were indifferent, seeking on all sides modes of active exertion, and for gleams of hope. She was, in the minds of all, so completely identified with Lord Russell that when he complained that the list of the jury had not been given to him beforehand, the Judge and the Attorney-

General considered it sufficient to prove that
Lady Russell had known their names. The
night before his appearance in court, she
wrote to him :—

"Your friends believe I can do you some
service at your trial. I am extremely willing to try. My resolution will hold out;
pray let yours. But it may be the court
will not let me. However, do you let me
try. I think, however, to meet you at
Richison's, and then resolve. Your brother
Ned will be with me, and sister Margaret."

The trial was on July 13, 1683. The
court was crowded with spectators : the
counsel complained that they had no room
to sit down. Lord Russell asked for pen,
ink, and paper, to take notes. They were
given to him. "May I have somebody to
help my memory?" he inquired. Permission
to have a servant to write for him was
given. "My wife," said he, "is here to do

it"; which being assented to, she took her place by his side, and continued her trying task through the day.

When sentence was passed, neither the courage nor the activity of Lady Russell ceased. She was one of those whose minds are supported by love, duty, and trust in God, beyond human anticipation, strength, and hope. Efforts of all kinds were made to save Lord Russell's life. Some of the most important men about the Court pleaded strongly with the King in his behalf. His release, they said, would impose a debt of gratitude on a powerful family; while, if their plea were rejected, the injury would never be forgotten. Moreover, some consideration was due to the daughter of Lord Southampton. From several quarters Lady Russell received intimations of steps which were being taken towards giving her an opportunity to throw herself at the feet of the King, who, it was thought, could not refuse her. The Duke of York as well as the King was appealed to. He listened quietly, and made no answer. The King impatiently said to Monmouth that he would have pardoned him, but then he must have broken with his brother. To Lord Dartmouth he answered, "All that is true; but it is also true that if I do not take his life, he will have mine." Other means were employed. Lord Bedford offered the Duchess of Portsmouth fifty and even a hundred thousand pounds, to obtain a pardon; but Charles answered that he would not sell his own blood, and that of his subjects, so cheaply. Lady Russell thought that her uncle, the Marquess de Ruvigny, might have some influence with Charles. The Marquess promised to come. Barillon, the French Ambassador, was instructed to speak to Charles in behalf of

Lord Russell; but when he did so, the
King said: "I am sure that the King, my
brother, would not advise me to pardon a
man who would have shown me no quarter.
I will not hinder M. de Ruvigny from
coming; but Lord Russell will lose his head
before he arrives. I owe this example for
my own safety and the good of the State."

Ruvigny did not come. At the urgent
request of his father, his friends, and even
of his wife, Lord Russell himself wrote to
the King, and to the Duke of York, request-
ing a pardon, declaring that he had never
entertained any designs against the King's
life, or even of overturning the Government,
and promising to go to live on the Continent
and to interfere no more in English affairs.
It was without any expectation of success
that he wrote these letters, and as he folded
up that for the Duke he said to Dr. Burnet,
" This will be printed and be selling about

the streets as my submission when I am hanged."

It was thought there might be one more chance—perhaps the best, though singular and indirect. Men's minds were strongly agitated by the question as to the possible legitimacy or the absolute illegitimacy of any armed resistance to the legitimate Sovereign. Man always desires to have reason on his side, and cannot rest in the mere possession of power if he feels that truth and justice are against him. Consequently, both the Court Party and the National Party claimed to be established on a principle, and to govern by right, not by power merely. The English Church maintained, without limitation, the illegality of resistance by force. Two of her moderate and most upright divines, Burnet and Tillotson, attempted to obtain Lord Russell's adherence to their doctrine, hoping to save his life if they could assure the King

on this point. At one time they thought
they had prevailed, and Lord Halifax, whom
they informed of the matter, told them that
when he reported it to the King, His
Majesty appeared to be more moved by this
prospect than by all the other applications.
They renewed their efforts. Lord Russell
listened to them quietly. Tillotson wrote
to him a letter arguing the maxim of non-
resistance as an article of Christian truth.
Lord Russell took the letter, retired into an
adjoining room, and, returning, said that he
should be glad to be convinced, but could
not say he was. He had always held that a
free nation had a right to defend its religion
and its liberties when they were assailed. If
he was in error, he hoped that God would
forgive him, as it would be a sin of ignorance.
Burnet still pressed the matter. Russell
answered that he could not tell a lie, and he
must if he went further. He had discussed

the question with his wife, who, far from urging him to give way, had sorrowfully approved and supported him in his firmness. It is said that she even showed some displeasure at Tillotson's urgency on the subject.

All means were vain;[1] all hopes successively died away; the fatal day was at hand. "I wish," said Lord Russell, "that my wife would give over beating every bush for my preservation"; but, considering that it would afterwards be a consolation to feel that she had done all that was in her power, he acquiesced. When they were together, they seemed to be each of them entirely occupied in strengthening and encouraging

[1] Lord Cavendish had nobly stood forward at the trial to vindicate Lord Russell's character, when it was deemed "almost as criminal to be a witness for him, as to have been an accomplice with him." After the sentence was passed, he offered to visit him in prison, change clothes with him, and remain in his place while he made his escape. Lord Russell, however, would not secure his own safety at the expense of his friend, nor injure the cause he had adopted by a course which would be construed as a confession of guilt.

the other ; when she left, he followed her with his eyes; his emotion seemed on the point of breaking forth ; he overcame it with difficulty, and gave himself up either alone, or with Burnet and Tillotson, to religious meditation, conversation, or reading. On July 19, being informed that the application for a respite till the following Monday had been rejected, and that the execution was fixed for the second day afterwards, he wrote a letter to the King which was not to be forwarded till after his death, in which he protested that he had always been devoted to what he believed to be the real interests of the Crown, and that if he had been mistaken he hoped that the King's displeasure would be satisfied by his death, and would not extend to his wife and children. On the following day, the 20th, he received the Sacrament from Tillotson.

"Do you believe all the articles of the

Christian faith as taught by the Church of England?" asked Tillotson.

"Yes."

"Do you forgive all your enemies?"

"With my whole heart."

After dinner, he read over and signed the paper which he intended to give to the Sheriff on the scaffold, as his farewell to life and to the country, and gave Lady Russell his instructions as to its publication and distribution immediately after his death. Lady Russell brought his children to him. He kept them with him for some time, conversed with her as to their education, and their prospects, kissed and blessed them, without losing his composure. "Stay and sup with me," he said to his wife. "Let us eat our last earthly food together." During and after supper he spoke cheerfully on various subjects, especially about his two girls, and mentioned several instances of men who had met death with calmness and firm minds. Towards ten o'clock he rose, took Lady Russell by the hand, and kissed her four or five times; both were silent and trembling, their eyes full of tears which did not over-flow. When she had left, " Now," said he to Burnet, " the bitterness of death is past"; and, suddenly giving himself up to his feelings, " What a blessing she has been to me, and what a misery it would have been if she had been crying to me to turn informer and to be a Lord Howard!" He said there was a signal providence of God in giving him such a wife, who brought rank, fortune, great understanding, great religion, and great kindness to him; but her carriage in his extremity was beyond all. Then he spoke of his own situation, and remarked how great a change death made, and how wonderfully these new scenes would strike on a soul. He had heard how some that had been born blind were struck when, by the couching of their cataracts, they saw; "but what," said he, "if the first thing they saw were the rising sun?"

In the morning, on his way to the place of execution, he sang to himself the 119th Psalm; and while preparing for the last blow he gave his watch to Burnet, saying, "I have done with time; now eternity comes." One of his last commissions was a kind message to his father's chaplain, Mr. Kettlewell, who held in their fullest extent opinions the opposite of those for which he was about to die.

CHAPTER V

LADY RUSSELL was now a widow, alone in her dwelling of Southampton House with her three children,—two girls, one nine years of age and the other seven, and a boy of three,—and it tends to excite some surprise that we find among the earliest of her letters, after so severe a blow, two addressed directly or indirectly to Charles II., who had just refused the life of her husband. Scarcely had she left London, whence she had retired with her children to her father-in-law the Earl of Bedford's seat at Woburn, when she wrote to her uncle, John Russell, Colonel of the 1st Regiment of Guards:

"Apologies, dear Uncle, are not necessary

to you for anything I do, nor is my dis-
composed mind fit to make any; but I want
your assistance, so I ask it freely. You may
remember, Sir, that a very few days after
my great and terrible calamity, the King
sent me word he meant to take no advantage
of anything that was forfeited to him, but
terms of law must be observed; so, now the
grant for the personal estate is done and in
my hands, I esteem it fit to make some compliment of acknowledgment to His Majesty;
to do this for me is the favour I beg of you;
but I have writ the enclosed paper in such a
manner that if you judge it fit, you may, as
you see cause, show it to the King, to let
him see what thanks I desire should be made
to him; but that is left to you to do as you
approve.

"Truly, Uncle, 'tis not without reluctancy
I write to you myself, since nothing that is
not very sad can come from me, and I do not

love to trouble such as, I am sure, wish me none. I ask after your health, and when I hear you are well, it is part of the only satisfaction I can have in this wretched world, where the love and company of the friends and nearest relations of that dear and blessed person must give me all I can find in it now; it is a great change from as much happiness as I believe this world can ever give, to know no more, as never must,—Yours,   R. RUSSELL."

Soon a rumour from Town reached Lady Russell in her retreat. She heard that the Court, disquieted by the effect produced on the country by the paper given to the Sheriff by Lord Russell on the scaffold, denied its authenticity. This roused her from her depression. She considered this attack an injury to her husband's memory, and hastened to write to the King in the style of a person called by a sense of duty to repel an injury to the dead, and seeming reckless of consequences to herself. The letter is endorsed "My Letter to the King, a Few Days After my Lord's Death," and is as follows:

"May it please Your Majesty,—I find my husband's enemies are not appeased with his blood, but still continue to misrepresent him to Your Majesty. It is a great addition to my sorrows to hear Your Majesty is prevailed upon to believe that the paper he delivered to the Sheriff at his death was not his own. I can truly say, and am ready in the solemnest manner to attest, that (during his imprisonment) I often heard him discourse the chiefest matters contained in that paper in the same expressions he therein uses, as some of those few relations that were admitted to him can likewise aver. And sure it is an argument of no great force that there is a phrase or two in it another uses, when nothing is more common than to take up such words we like, or are accustomed to in our conversation. I beg leave further to avow to Your Majesty, that all that is set down in the paper read to Your Majesty on Sunday night, to be spoken in my presence, is exactly true; as I doubt not but the rest of the paper is, which was written at my request; and the author of it, in all his conversation with my husband that I was privy to, showed himself a loyal subject to Your Majesty, a faithful friend to him, and a most tender and conscientious minister to his soul. I do, therefore, humbly beg Your Majesty would be so charitable to believe that he, who in all his life was observed to act with the greatest clearness and sincerity, would not at the point of death do so disingenuous and false a thing as to deliver for his own what was not properly and expressly so. And if, after the loss in such a manner of the best husband in the world, I were capable of any consolation, Your Majesty only could afford it by having better thoughts of him, which, when I was so importunate to speak with Your Majesty, I thought I had some reason to believe I should have inclined you to, not from the credit of my word, but upon the evidence of what I had to say. I hope I have written nothing in this that will displease Your Majesty. If I have, I humbly beg of you to consider it as coming from a woman amazed with grief; and that you will pardon the daughter of a person who served Your Majesty's father in his greatest extremities (and Your Majesty in your greatest posts), and one that is not conscious of having ever done anything to offend you (before). I shall ever pray for Your Majesty's long life and happy reign—Who am with all humility, May it please Your Majesty,

"R. RUSSELL."

It is a widow aggrieved, it is the devoted
wife of a conspirator just dead on the scaffold
for maintaining the right of resistance and
the liberties of his country, who manifests
with such simplicity this profound respect
for Monarchy, this attention to propriety,
this susceptibility so humble in words, so
proud in reality. Days, months, years, pass
on ; she remains the same, entirely given to
one feeling, without being overwhelmed by
it ; at the same time collected, attentive, and
even active, in the business of life. Her
friend Dr. Fitzwilliam takes the most tender
interest in the noble daughter of his old
patron, and employs his uttermost efforts to
support, to console, to lead her through all
her troubles closer to her God and Saviour.
It is to him that Lady Russell opens her
heart ; it is to him she confides all her
internal conflicts—her fits of depression, her
seasons of trustful confidence. The follow-

ing extracts from this correspondence will be sufficient to give some idea of her character, especially rare and admirable inasmuch as passion and good sense, tenderness of feeling and firmness of mind, never neutralise each other. Through forty years of widowhood, whilst devoted to the memory of a beloved husband, she continued reasonable and active in all the relations, all the affections, all the duties,—we might almost say, all the interests,—of the world around her.

Shortly after her misfortune, Dr. Fitzwilliam had sent her some religious advice, and forms of prayer. In her answer she says:

"I need not tell you, good Doctor, how little capable I have been of such an exercise as this. You will soon find how unfit I am still for it, since my yet disordered thoughts can offer me no other than such words as express the deepest sorrows, and confused as my yet amazed mind is. But such men as you, and particularly one so much my friend, will, I know, bear with my weakness and compassionate my distress, as you have already done by your good letter and excellent prayer. I endeavour to make the best use I can of both ; but I am so evil and unworthy a creature, that though I have desires, yet I have no dispositions or worthiness, towards receiving comfort. You that know us both and how we lived, must allow I have just cause to bewail my loss. I know it is common with others to lose a friend ; but to have lived with such a one, it may be questioned how few can glory in the like happiness, so consequently lament the like loss. Who can but shrink at such a blow, till by the mighty aids of His Holy Spirit, we will let the gift of God, which He hath put into our hearts, interpose ? That reason which sets a measure to our souls in prosperity will then suggest many things which we have seen and heard to moderate us in such sad circumstances as mine. But, alas! my understanding is clouded, my faith weak, sense strong, and the devil busy to fill my thoughts with false notions, difficulties, and doubts . . . but this I hope to make matter of humiliation, not sin."

A few days later:

"You deal with me, Sir, just as I would be dealt withal; and it is possible I feel the more smart from my raging griefs because I would not take them off, but upon fit considerations; as it is easiest to our natures to have our sore in deep wounds gently handled; yet as most profitable, I would yield, nay desire, to have mine searched, that, as you religiously design by it, they may not fester. It is possible I grasp at too much of this kind, for a spirit so broke by affliction; for I am so

jealous that time, or necessity, the ordinary
abater of all violent passions (nay, even employment, or company of such friends as I
have left), should do that my reason or religion ought to do, as makes me covet the
best advices, and use all methods to obtain
such a relief as I can ever hope for, a silent
submission to the severe and terrible providence, without any ineffective unwillingness
to bear what I must suffer; and such a
victory over myself, that, when once allayed,
immoderate passions may not be apt to break
out again upon fresh occasions and accidents,
offering to my memory that dear object of
my desires, which must happen every day, I
may say every hour, of the longest life I can
live, that so, when I must return into the
world, so far as to act that part is incumbent
upon me in faithfulness to him I owe as
much as can be due to man, it may be with
great strength of spirits, and grace to live a

stricter life of holiness to my God, who will
not always let me cry to Him in vain. On
Him I will wait till He have pity on me,
humbly imploring that, by the mighty aids of
His most Holy Spirit, He will touch my heart
with greater love to Himself. Then I shall
be what He would have me. But I am unworthy of such spiritual blessing, who remain
so unthankful a creature for those earthly
ones I have enjoyed, because I have them no
longer. Yet God, who knows our frames, will
not expect that when we are weak we should
be strong. This is much comfort under my
deep dejections, which are surely increased
by the subtle malice of that great enemy of
souls, taking all advantages upon my present
weakened and wasted spirits, assaulting with
divers temptations, as, when I have in any
measure overcome one kind, I find another
in the room, as when I am less afflicted (as I
before complained), then I find reflections

troubling me, as omissions of some sort or other; that if either greater persuasions had been used, he had gone away; or some errors at the trial amended, or other applications made, he might have been acquitted, and so yet have been in the land of the living (though I discharge not these things as faults upon myself, yet as aggravations to my sorrows); so that not being certain of our time being appointed, beyond which we cannot pass, my heart shrinks to think his time possibly was shortened by unwise management, I believe I do ill to torment myself with such unprofitable thoughts."

To Mr. Griffith, who had written to her on occasion of her loss, she writes:

"I have loved man too well, and did not weigh enough how short my interest might be in that loved object of my desires: had God had full possession of my soul, or had I prized His love, adored His wisdom, and

believed His goodness in all the secret con-
ducts of His providences (yea, although I
groaned under the sharpest dispensations of
it), I should not be cast down; but passion
rebels, and I cannot, with the constancy and
frame of spirit I desire, follow His steps in
that thorny path of suffering He trod before
me with so much ease: this calls for the
sharpest accents of my lamentations; but I
still bestow them upon the loss of earthly
enjoyments; our grosser part lying nearer to
their more suitable objects in the mixed state
of this world; sense soon prevails, and by
perpetual sharp and quick remembrances
brings to my mind how full of content my
mind lately was, and that I must never here
know more; it is a bitter reflective, can only
be allayed by seriously fixing upon that consideration you have lighted on to offer me,
that whatever he did in his place he did it
faithfully, as unto God, and upon that belief

may safely ground a hope he was lifted from
a prison to a throne; then I know it is very
unreasonable to take so heavily, that what
was so precious to me, his gain, should be
matter of so grievous and lasting a weight
of sorrow to me; but I must hope this is my
infirmity, and that our High Priest, who was
touched with ours, will give me (who with
my soul desires with my groans to mingle
justification of my God) suffering grace for a
suffering condition, making His rod medicinal
to me; and by giving a strong faith in the
precious promises of the gospel, I shall one
day be able to evidence to my soul, that they
belong to me, that His rod and love have
gone together, and, though sorely chastened,
yet instruction hath accompanied correction,
awakened and quickened me to make my
calling and election sure, bearing up my
evidence to heaven, where, after a few more
weary days, we shall together enjoy the

visions of God, ever praising Him to eternal
ages, without interposition of ill accidents:
that I may prepare for this blessed change,
and without undue impatience wait the time,
and in the meanwhile attain such a measure
of comfort as is necessary for a prudent and
faithful discharge of my remaining duty to
him to whom I owe as much as can be due
to man. Remember me, good Mr. Griffith,
in your supplications to the Throne of Grace
for suitable divine assistance to the miseries
and necessities of, Sir, your ever sad but
faithful friend to serve you,

" R. RUSSELL."

CHAPTER VI

FOR some time after her efforts in behalf of her husband and her loss, there was a reaction and depression which threatened to become permanent, and in some measure to disable her from feeling the consolations of religion. Dr. Fitzwilliam seems to have remonstrated with her on having indulged her feelings by visiting her husband's tomb. She answered:

"Doctor, I had considered I went not to seek the living among the dead; I knew I should not see him any more wherever I went, and had made a covenant with myself, not to break out in unreasonable, fruitless passion, but quicken my contemplation whither the nobler part was fled, to a country afar off, where no earthly power bears any sway, nor can put an end to a happy society; there I would willingly be, but we must not limit our time : I hope to wait without impatiency."

In another letter she says :

"But sure, Doctor, it is the nature of sorrow to lay hold on all things which give a new ferment to it; then how could I choose but feel it in a time of so much confusion as these last weeks have been, closing so tragically as they have done; and sure never any poor creature for two whole years together has had more awakers to quicken and revive the anguish of soul than I have had; yet I hope I do most truly desire that nothing may be so bitter to me, as to think that I have in the least offended thee, O my God, and that nothing may be so marvellous in my eyes as the exceeding love of my

Lord Jesus; that, heaven being my aim, and the longing expectations of my soul, I may go through honour and dishonour, good report and bad report, prosperity and adversity, with some evenness of mind. The inspiring me with these desires is, I hope, a token of His never-failing love towards me though an unthankful creature for all the good things I have enjoyed, and do still in the lives of hopeful children by so beloved a husband."

Again :

"You cannot make so great a mistake, good Doctor, I know, as not to be assured I accept most kindly every method you take for the disposing my sad heart to be submissively content with my position here; and then to revive it to some thankful temper by various reflections. I do not resist so foolishly as to say they are not proper ones; I can discern so justly as to

know you do not err, Doctor, in the manner
of magnifying your charitable respect, nor
in the design nor prosecution of it; the
virtue you chiefly recommend to practise is
so beautifully set forth, it is as a burning
shining light, and one is willing to live with
that light. But my languishing, weary spirit
rises up slowly to all good: yet I hope by
God's abundant grace in time your labours
will work the same effect in my spirit; they
will indeed in less time on others better
disposed and prepared than I am, who in
the day of affliction seem to have no remembrance, with due thankfulness, of prosperity.
Your papers, sure, Sir, are rarely fitted for
the use of all struggling under the burden
of sin or sorrow, though by a singular and
particular charity composed for my lamentable calamity, and as seasonably is this new
supply come, as is possible, for its first
perusal by me. Since I unsealed your

packet this very morning, the 21st of July, a day of bitterness indeed, I seasoned the first minutes of retirement, I allotted this day for prayer and mourning, with reading them, and made a stop for some time on those lines—'We may securely depend on the truth of God's promises, to this purpose, that a seed-time of tears shall be followed by a plenteous harvest of joys.' It is a sound I must hereafter be a stranger to in my pilgrimage here, but that it shall one day belong to me is a contemplation of great comfort, and I bless God it is so; I must not in lowliness 'of mind deny the grace I sometimes feel, though faint are my best thoughts and performances, as I am sensible."

After passing ten months at Woburn, in solitude and inaction, she felt the need of change of scene, and of seeking new impressions. On April 20, 1684, she wrote:

"The future part of my life will not, I

expect, pass as perhaps I would just choose ;
sense has been long enough gratified, indeed
so long I know not how to live by faith ;
yet the pleasant stream that fed it near
fourteen years together being gone, I have
no sort of refreshment but when I can repair
to that living fountain from whence all
flows ; while I look not at the things which
are seen, but at those which are not seen,
expecting that day which will settle and
compose all my tumultuous thoughts in
perpetual peace and quiet ; but am undone,
irrecoverably so, as to my temporal longings
and concerns. Time runs on and usually
wears off some of that sharpness of thought
inseparable from my circumstances, but I
cannot experience such an effect ; every
week making me more and more sensible
of the miserable change in my condition : but
the same merciful hand which has held me
up from sinking in the extremest calamities,

will (I verily believe) do so still, that I faint
not, to the end in this sharp conflict, nor
add sin to my grievous weight of sorrows,
by too high a discontent, which is all I have
now to fear. You do, I doubt not, observe
I let my pen run too greedily upon this
subject; indeed it is very hard upon me to
restrain it, especially to such as pity my
distress, and would assist towards my relief
any way in their power. I am glad I have
so expressed myself to you, as to fix you in
resolving to continue the course you have
begun with me, which is to set before me
plainly my duty in all kinds: it was my
design to engage you to it; nor shall you
be less successful with me, in your desires,
could there happen occasion for it, which
is most unlikely, Dr. Fitzwilliam understanding himself and the world so well.
On neither of the points, I believe, I shall
give you reason to complain, yet please

myself in both, so far of one mind we shall be.

"I am entertaining some thoughts of going to that now desolate place Stratton, for a few days, where I must expect new amazing reflections at first, it being a place where I have lived in full and sweet content, considered the condition of others, and thought none deserved my envy; but I must pass no more such days on earth; however, plans are indeed nothing. Where can I dwell that his figure is not present to me? Nor would I have it otherwise; so I resolve that shall be no bar, if it proves requisite for the better acquitting any obligation upon me. That which is the immediate one is settling, and indeed giving up, the trust my dear Lord had from my best sister. Fain would I see that performed, as I know he would have done it had he lived. If I find I can do as I desire in it, I will (by God's permission) infallibly go ; but indeed not to stay more than two or three weeks, my children remaining here, who shall ever have my diligent attendance, therefore shall hasten back to them."

Five months later :

" I have resolved to try that desolate habitation of mine at London this winter. The doctor agrees it is the best place for my boy, and I have no argument to balance that, nor could take the resolution to see London till that was urged ; but by God's permission I will try how I can endure that place, in thought a place of terror to me ; but I know if sorrow had not another root, that will vanish in a few days."

She did not carry out her intention immediately, and six weeks afterwards she wrote :

" I have, you find, Sir, lingered out my time here, and I think none will wonder at it, that will reflect the place I am going to remove to was the scene of so much lasting sorrow to me, and where I acted so unsuccessful a part for the preservation of a life I could sure have laid down mine to have continued. It was, Doctor, an inestimable treasure I did lose, and with whom I had lived in the highest pitch of the world's felicity. But I must remember I have a better Friend, a more abiding, whom I desire with an inflamed heart to know, not alone as good in a way of profit, but amiable in a way of excellency; then spiritual joy will grapple with earthly griefs, and so far overcome as to give some tranquillity to a mind so tossed to and fro as mine has been with the evils of this life; yet I have but the experience of short moments of this desirable temper, and fear to have fewer when I first come to that desolate habitation and place where so many passions will assault me : but having so many months mourned the substance, I think (by God's assistance) the shadows will not sink me."

Her hope was fulfilled. Though often falling into fits of despondency or weakness, she overcame them, and her firmness of mind and fervent piety kept her from exaggerated feelings for the present, or fears in regard to the future. She writes, a few months after the foregoing :

"I strive to reflect how large my portion of good things has been ; and though they are passed away no more to return, yet I have a pleasant work to do, dress up my soul for my desired change, and fit it for the converse of angels and the spirits of just men made perfect, amongst whom my hope is my loved Lord is one ; and my often repeated prayer to my God is, that if I have a reasonable ground for that hope, it may give a refreshment to my poor soul."

A few months later:

" The great thing is to acquiesce with all one's heart to the good pleasure of God, who will prove us by the ways and dispensations He sees best; and when He will break us to pieces we must be broken. Who can tell His works from the beginning to the end? But who can praise His mercies more than wretched I, that He has not cut me off in anger, who have taken His chastisements so heavily, not weighing His mercies in the midst of judgments? The stroke was of the fiercest, sure; but had I not then a reasonable ground to hope that what I loved as I did my own soul was raised from a prison to a throne? Was I not enabled to shut up my own sorrows, that I increased not his sufferings by seeing mine?"

Again, still a few months later:

" I cannot tell, Doctor, whether your papers met me in a better temper now, than at some other times, to relish them; yet

7

sure I esteem these sheets to be so fine, that it brought into my mind the loss you have lately sustained of a much-loved friend; and to conclude, that a new experience of grief had, in your struggles to overcome all unfit discontent, raised your fancy to the highest pitch of framing arguments against it; it is a happy effect of sorrow, and a sure evidence to the soul that the promises of the Holy Word belong to her; that the work of grace is apt, and grows towards those degrees where, when we arrive, we shall triumph over imperfections, and our wills desire nothing but what shall please God. We shall, as your phrase is, be renewed like eagles; and we, like eagles, mount up to meet the Lord coming in the clouds, and ever tarry with Him, and be no more faint or weary in God's service. These are ravishing contemplations, Doctor! They clasp the heart with delight for such moments, or, to say

more truly, part of a moment, that the soul
is so well fixed. It is true, we can (you are
sure) bear the occasions of grief without
being sunk and drowned in those passions ;
but to bear them without a murmuring heart—
there is the task ; and in failing—there lies
the sin. O Lord, lay it not to the charge of
thy weak servant ; but make me cheerfully
thankful that I had such a friend to lose ;
and contented that he has had dismission
from his attendance here (an expression you
use I am much pleased with). When my time
comes that I shall have mine, I know not how
it will find me then ; but I am sure it is my best
reviving thought now ; when I am plunged
in multitudes of wild and sad thoughts, I
recover and recollect a little time will end
this life, and begin a better that shall never '
end, and where we shall discover the reasons
and ends of all those seeming severe providences we have known. Thus I seem to

long for the last day, and yet it is possible if sickness, or other forerunner of our dissolution, were present, I would defer it if I could; so deceitful are our hearts, or so weak is our faith. But I think, one may argue again, that God has wisely implanted in our nature a shrinking at the approach of a separation; and that may make us content, if not desire a delay. If it were not so implanted there, many would not endure the evils of life that now do it, though they are taught duty that obliges us thereto."

A year later:

"I had made him my idol, though I did not know it; I loved man too much and God too little; yet my constant prayer was not to do so—but not enough fervent I doubt. I will turn the object of my love all I can upon his loved children, and if I may be directed and blessed in their education, what is it I have to ask in relation to this perishing world for myself? It is joy and peace in believing that I covet, having nothing to fear but sin.

" The near and pleasing concern you make the well-being of me and mine to be to you, I believe most hearty and sincere, and kindly engages me to great thankfulness; but amongst your choicest expressions, you are induced to say you could rather envy my condition than pity it, from an opinion of being supported and comforted with a well-grounded persuasion of my having a right and title to those precious promises that will give a pleasant and perpetual rest to the weary and heavy-laden soul. This, Doctor, is perhaps what you mistake in; and I have led you into the error by speaking too well of my own thoughts or exercises, which are truly all mean and encompassed with un-comfortable weakness; yet I have not the confusion to reflect I have said anything from a false glory; I should, if I can discern right,

wrong my own heart by it, and that grace
of God which disposes me, though in the
meanest degree, to ask for and thirst after
such comforts as the world cannot give.
What it can give I am most sure I have
felt, and experienced them uncertain and
perishing; such I will never more (grace
assisting) look after; and yet I expect a
joyful day, after some more sorrowful ones;
and though I walk sadly through the valley
of death, I will fear no evil, humbling myself
under the mighty hand of God, who will save
me in the day of trouble; He knows my
sorrows and the weakness of my person.　I
commit myself and mine to Him.

"The pensive quiet I hope for here
[Woburn], I think, will be very grateful to
my weary body and mind; yet when I con-
template the fruits of the trial and labour of
these last six months,[1] it brings some comfort

---

[1] The marriage of her eldest daughter.

to my mind, as an evidence that I do not live only to lament my misfortunes, and be humbled by those heavy chastisements I have felt, which must for ever in this life press me sorely. That I have not sunk under the pressure has been, I hope, in mercy, that I might be better fitted for my eternal state, and form the children of a loved husband before I go hence. With these thoughts I can be hugely content to live; and the rather as the clouds seem to gather and threaten storms; though God only knows how I may acquit myself, and what help I may be, or what example I shall give to my young creatures. I mean well towards them, if I know my heart."

The following was written two years later:

"By report I fear poor Lady Gainsborough is in new trouble; for though she has all the help of religion to support her,

yet that does not shut us out from all sorrow;
it does not direct us to insensibility if we
could command it, but to a quiet submission
to the will of God, making His ours as
much as we can.   Indeed, Doctor, you are
extremely in the right to think that my life
has been so embittered, it is now a very
poor thing to me : yet, I find myself careful
enough of it.   I think I am useful to my
children, and would endure hard things to
do for them till they can do for themselves ;
but alas! I am apt to conclude if I had not
that, yet I should still find out some reason
to be content to live, though I am weary of
everything and of the folly, the vanity, and
the madness of man most of all.   There is
a shrinking from the separation of the soul
from the body, that is implanted in our
natures, which enforces us to conserve life ;
and it is a wise Providence ; for who would
else endure much evil, that is not taught the

great advantage of patient sufferings ? I am heartily sorry, good Doctor, that you are not exempt, which I am sure you are not, when you cannot exercise your care as formerly among your flock at Cottenham. But I will not enlarge on this matter, nor any other at this time."

After another two years she writes :

" But to come to the purpose of yours, which I received the 13th of this lamentable month, the very day of that hard sentence pronounced against my dear friend and husband : it was the fast day, and so I had the opportunity of retiring without any taking notice of it, which pleases me best. What shall I say, Doctor ? That I do live by your rules? No: I should lie. I bless God it has long been my purpose, with some endeavour, through mercy, to do it. I hope I may conclude I grieve without sinning ; yet I cannot attain to that love of God, and submission to all His providences, that I can rejoice in; however, I bless Him for His infinite mercy, in a support that is not wrought from the world (though my heart is too much bound up in the blessings I have yet left); and I hope chiefly He has enabled me to rejoice in Him as my everlasting portion, and in the assured hope of good things in the other world.

"Good Doctor, we are travelling the same way, and hope, through mercy, to meet at the same happy end of all our labours here, in an eternal rest: and it is of great advantage to that attainment, communicating pious thoughts to each other; nothing on this side heaven goes so near to it; and being where God is, it is heaven. If He be in our hearts there will be peace and satisfaction, when one recollects the happiness of such a state (which, if my heart deceives me not, I hope is mine), and I will try to experience more and more that blessed promise—'Come unto me, all ye that are heavy laden, and I will give you ease.' This day and this subject inclines me to be very long, and might to another be too tedious; but I know it is not so to Dr. Fitzwilliam, who uses to feast in the house of mourning. However, my time to open my chamber door is near, and I take some care not to affect in these retirements."

CHAPTER VII

THE foregoing excerpts show how Lady
Russell attempted to resist the depression
to which her circumstances naturally gave
rise. She received many letters of consolation and friendly counsel from Burnet,
Tillotson, Patrick, Howe, and others; for
which in one of her letters she expresses
her gratitude:

" How were my sinking spirits supported
by the early compassions of excellent and
wise Christians, without ceasing, admonish-
ing me of my duty, instructing, reproving,
comforting me! You know, Doctor, I was
not destitute; and I must acknowledge that
many others like yourself, with devout zeal

and charity, contributed to the gathering together of my scattered spirits, and then subjecting them by reason to such submission as I could obtain under so astonishing a calamity."

She wrote also, if not with the same freedom, at least with the same sentiments, to some persons who had rendered her important services, or shown her sympathy under her trial. Lord Halifax, among others, had interceded with the King, after the execution of Lord Russell, and had obtained, with great difficulty, permission that his family arms might be placed over the door of his house, as if he had died a natural death. He had subsequently maintained a friendly relation with Lady Russell, who wrote to him on the death of his daughter Lady Carbery in 1689. Lord Halifax, in acknowledging her letter, had given expression to his feelings at some political vexations which had annoyed him about the same time; on which Lady Russell wrote again as follows :

"My Lord,—For my part, I think the man a very indifferent reasoner, that to do well he must take with indifference whatever happens to him. It is very fine to say, Why should we complain that is taken back which was but lent us, and lent us but for a time, we know ? and so on. They are the receipts of philosophers I have no reverence for, as I have not for anything which is unnatural. It is insincere. And I dare say they did dissemble, and felt what they would not own. I know I cannot dispute with Almighty Power; but yet if my delight is gone, I must needs be sorry it is taken away, according to the measure it made me glad.

"The Christian religion only, believe me, my Lord, has a power to make the spirit

easy under great calamity ; nothing less than
the hope of being again made happy can
satisfy the mind : I am sure I owe more to
it than I could have done to the world, if
all the glories of it had been offered me,
or to be disposed of by me. And I do
sincerely desire your Lordship may experience the truth of my opinion. You
know better than most, from the share you
have had of the one, what they do afford ;
and I hope you will prove what tranquillity
the other gives. If I had a better wish to
make, your Lordship's constant expressions
of esteem for me, and willingness, as I hope,
to have had me less miserable than I am,
if you had found your power equal to your
will, engages me to make it ; and that alone
would have bound me, though my own
unworthiness and ill fortune had let you
have forgot me for ever after my sad lot.
But since you would not do so, it must

deserve a particular acknowledgment for ever."

A distressing but efficacious diversion of her thoughts was given her by a near prospect of fresh losses. Her son, scarcely four years old, became dangerously ill. She was on the point of losing him; but he recovered.

"God has been pitiful to my small grace," she wrote to Dr. Fitzwilliam, "and removed a threatened blow, which must have quickened my sorrows, if not added to them,—the loss of my poor boy. He has been ill, and God has let me see the folly of my imaginations, which made me apt to conclude I had nothing left the deprivation of which could be matter of much anguish, or its possession of any considerable refreshment. I have felt the falseness of the first notion, for I know not how to part with tolerable ease from the little creature. I desire to do so of the second, and that my thankfulness for the real blessing of these children may refresh my weary, labouring mind with some joy and satisfaction, at least in my endeavours to do that part towards them their most dear and tender father would not have omitted, and which, if successful, though early made unfortunate, may conduce to their happiness for the time to come and hereafter. When I have done this piece of duty to my best friend and them, how gladly would I lie down by that beloved dust I lately went to visit (that is, the case that holds it)."

Shortly afterwards:

"You hear I am at Totteridge, and why I came thither, and soon will know I wanted the auxiliaries you took care to send me; sure I did so, but it hath pleased the Author of all Mercies to give me some glimpse and ray of His compassions in this dark day of my calamity, the child being exceedingly better; and I trust no secret murmur or discontent at what I have felt, and must still do, shall provoke my God to repeat those threatenings of making yet more bitter that cup I have drunk so deeply out of; but as a quiet submission is required under all the various methods of Divine Providence, I trust I shall be so supported, that though unfit thoughts may haunt me, they shall not break in importunately upon me, nor will I break off that bandage time will lay over my wound. To them that seek the Lord His mercies are renewed every morning; with all my strength to Him I will seek; and though He kill me I will trust in Him; my hopes are not of this world; I can never more recover pleasure here; but more durable joys I shall obtain, if I persevere to the end of a short life."

Three years later she writes:

" I often think, could but this single particular be fixed firmly in our hearts, that God knows where it is best to place His creatures, and is good to all, delighting not to punish what He has made, how easily and safely could we live by rule, and despise the world; not as, perhaps, I do, because I cannot recover what was a perpetual bliss to me here, but as considering we are strangers and pilgrims upon earth, travelling to a better country, and therefore may well bear with bad accommodations sometimes in our way to it. None are so dealt with, I believe, as not to live some days of joy, yet we can lay no claim to do so, nor are the happiest here below without tasting the bitter cup of affliction at some time of their life; so imperfect is this state, and doubtless wisely and mercifully ordered so, that through all the changes and chances of this mortal life we may be the most apt to thrust forward towards, and in the end (with inexpressible joy) attain, that state where, as you express it, we shall feel no more storms, but enjoy a perpetual calm. What can be more? The thought clasps one's heart, and causes the imprisoned soul to long to take her flight! But it is our duty to wait with patience each of us our appointed time."

She had long to wait for the happy re-union which she so strongly desired. While waiting, as years passed on, she treated her grief as men treat an ailment which cannot be cured, with which they learn to live. Notwithstanding the void in her heart, her life was active, and she was occupied without her thoughts being distracted. The education of her children, their prospects, the management of her household, the interests and welfare of her neighbours, were the objects of her constant care. "I am very glad," wrote Burnet, "that you intend to

employ so much of your time in the education
of your children, that they shall need no
other governess ; for as it is the greatest
part of your duty, so it will be a noble
entertainment to you, and the best diversion
and cure of your wounded and wasted
spirits." Her daughters, indeed, never had
any other governess. She was careful that
her own sorrow should not interfere with
enjoyments proper to their age.

" The poor children," she wrote, when
she returned to Stratton, " are well pleased
to be a little while in a new place, ignorant
how much better it has been both to me and
them ; yet I thought I found Rachel not
insensible, and I could not but be content
with it in my mind. Those whose age can
afford them any remembrance should,
methinks, have some solemn thoughts for so
irreparable a loss to themselves and family ;
though after that I would cherish a cheerful

temper in them with all the industry I can ; for sure we please our Maker best when we take all His providences with a cheerful spirit."

She bore a most grateful affection to her father-in-law, the Earl of Bedford. He lost his wife.[1] She gave up a journey she had designed, and remained with him. " I would not choose," she said, " to leave a good man under a new oppression of sorrow, that has been, and is, so very tender to me." It was to her that application was made amid all important circumstances connected with the family : among others, in a project for the marriage of her brother-in-law, Edward Russell, and one of the daughters of Lord

[1] Anne, daughter and sole heiress of Robert Carr, Earl of Somerset, by his too celebrated Countess, Frances Howard, the divorced wife of Essex. The Earl's father strongly objected to the marriage, saying that his son might take any other woman in England. His consent was obtained only by the King's interference. Lady Bedford's health never recovered the shock which it had received from her son's execution ; and her death is said to have been hastened by the accidental sight of a pamphlet commenting on her mother's guilt, the knowledge of which had been carefully kept from her. She was found senseless with it open before her.

Gainsborough, father-in-law of her sister
Elizabeth; and a proposal made by Lord
Strafford for one of her sisters-in-law. It
was known that her advice would be good,
and that her approval would carry great
weight. "I have done it," she writes on one
of these occasions, "though I wish she had
made choice of any other person than myself,
who, desiring to know the world no more, am
utterly unfitted for the management of anything in it; but must, as I can, engage in
such necessary offices for my children as I
cannot be dispensed from, nor desire to be,
since it is an eternal obligation upon me to
the memory of a husband to whom, and to
his, I have dedicated the few and sad
remainder of my days in this vale of misery
and trouble."

CHAPTER VIII

THE day of so much interest for mothers arrived sooner than she expected. Her eldest daughter, Rachel, was only fourteen when Lord Cavendish, Earl of Devonshire, asked her in marriage for his eldest son, who was only sixteen. Lord Cavendish had been the most intimate and devoted friend of Lord Russell;[1] and Lady Russell, feeling deeply the sentiment which dictated the proposal, and sensible of the fitness of the connection, accepted it with much satisfaction.

"I trust," she wrote to Dr. Fitzwilliam, "if I perfect this great work, my careful endeavours will prosper; only the Almighty

[1] See p. 65.

knows what the event shall be; but sure it is a glimmering of light I did not look for in my dark day. I do often repeat in my thoughts, The children of the just shall be blessed: I am persuaded their father was such: and if my heart deceive me not, I intend the being so, and humbly bless God for it."

The settlements were difficult to arrange: the most exalted sentiments are sometimes united with sordid and obstinate requirements.

"I have," wrote Lady Russell, "a well-bred lord to deal with, yet inflexible, if the point is not to his advantage. I am to meet him this morning at eleven o'clock at the lawyer's chambers, proposing to give a finishing stroke to the agreement between us, and then the deeds will be drawn in a few more weeks, I hope, and the matter perfected."

These conferences and discussions annoyed her. "I meet," she said, " with hard difficulties in the lawyer's hands; we are forced to be with a great many of that profession, which is very troublesome at this time to me, who would fain be delivered from them, conclude my affairs, and so put some period to that inroad methinks I make on my intended manner of living the rest of my days on earth. But I hope my duty shall always prevail above the strongest inclination I have. I believe to assist my yet helpless children is my business; which makes me take many dinners abroad, and do of that nature many things the performance of which is hard enough to a heavy and weary mind; but yet, I bless God, I do it."

She brought these affairs to an end, however; and on 21st June 1688 her daughter was married to the young Lord Cavendish, who almost immediately departed to travel on the Continent.

It would be a mistake to suppose that

Lady Russell lived strictly in retirement, with her sweet but sad memories, her religious meditations, her duties and family cares. She was not naturally of a very lively and fertile mind; nor was she disposed spontaneously to seek and to find everywhere subjects of interest and action. Left to herself and to ordinary life, she would perhaps have taken no part in the great ideas and movements of the time; but she had entered into them in company with her husband, from sympathy with him, and with a mind capable of understanding and feeling everything great. She continued faithful to Lord Russell's cause as to his memory, and constantly occupied, in her isolated state, with the same questions of religious and political liberties which, had he been still with her, would have formed the subjects of their joint solicitude and of their private conversation. The revocation of the Edict of Nantes excited in her not only the most lively sympathy with the proscribed Protestants, but also deep moral reflections.   In writing to Dr. Fitzwilliam she said:

" Doctor, I will take your advice, and vie my state with others, and begin with him in the highest prosperity, as himself thinks, the King of a miserable people; but truly the most miserable himself, by debasing as he does the dignity of human nature; and though, for secret ends of Providence, he is suffered to make these poor creatures drink deep of a most bitter cup, yet the dregs are surely reserved for himself.   What a judgment it is upon an aspiring mind, when perhaps half the world knows not God nor confesses the name of Christ as a Saviour, nor the beauty of virtue, which almost all the world has in derision, that it should not excite him to a reformation of faith and manners; but with such a rage turn his power to extirpate a people that own the Gospel for their law and rule! How infamous to his fame is the one! How glorious to his memory would the other have been! But he is too wicked to be an instrument of so much good to his degenerate age. Now, Sir, I cannot choose but think myself less miserable than this poor King. For the vast numbers of sufferers, the sound thereof is more terrible to those at a distance than the calamity of a single person; but taken asunder, the sufferings of any one, and those I have and do feel, are not perhaps at so wide a distance as it appears, theirs being heaped together; but, as you very well note, there is no state to be pronounced extremely miserable, but a state of sin, which will deprive us of a future state of glory, without a deep repentance, which I wish to all sinners. I hear our King has given leave for collection for those

Protestants which have been drove hither. God make His people thankful for it."

Two months later she says :

" Yesterday the Lord Delamere passed his trial, and was acquitted. I do bless God that He has caused some stop to the effusion of blood that has been shed of late in this poor land. But, Doctor, as diseased bodies turn the best nourishments, and even cordials, into the same sour humour that consumes and eats them up, just so do I. When I should rejoice with them that do rejoice, I seek a corner to weep in, I find I am capable of no more gladness ; but every new circumstance, the very comparing my night of sorrow after such a day with theirs of joy, does, from a reflection of one kind or other, rack my uneasy mind. Though I am far from wishing the close of theirs like mine, yet I cannot refrain giving some time to lament mine was not like theirs ; but I certainly took too much delight in my lot, and would too willingly have built my tabernacle here, for which I hope my punishment will end with life.

"The accounts from France are more and more astonishing; the perfecting work is vigorously pursued, and by this time completed, it is thought; all without exception having a day given them; only those I am going to mention have found so much grace as I'll tell you. . . . It is enough to sink the strongest heart to read the relations are sent over. How the children are torn from their mothers and sent into monasteries, their mothers to another. The husband to prison or the galley. These are amazing providences, Doctor! God out of infinite mercy strengthen weak believers! I am too melancholy an intelligencer to be very long, so will hasten to conclude."

Her own country engaged her attention in a still greater degree. The trial and

death of Algernon Sidney, the succession
of James II., the progress of his tyranny,
Monmouth's insurrection, and the severities
then inflicted on so many of the friends of
the cause which was dear to her, revived
her most painful remembrances.   At times
she derived an unexpected consolation even
from these misfortunes.

"The new scenes of each day," she
writes, "make me often conclude myself
very void of temper and reason, that I
still shed tears of sorrow, and not of joy,
that so good a man is landed safe on the
happy shore of a blessed eternity; doubtless
he is at rest, though I find none without him,
so true a partner he was in all my joys and
griefs; I trust the Almighty will pass by
this my infirmity; I speak it in respect to
the world, from whose enticing delights I
can now be better weaned.   I was too rich
in possession while I possessed him; all

relish now is gone. I bless God for it, and
pray and ask of all good people (do it for me
from such you know are so) also to pray
that I may more and more turn the stream
of my affection upwards, and set my heart
upon the ever-satisfying perfections of God ;
not starting at His darkest providences, but
remembering continually either His glory,
justice, or power is advanced by every one
of them, and that mercy is over all His
works, as we shall one day with ravishing
delight see. In the meantime I endeavour
to suppress all wild imaginations a melancholy fancy is apt to let in, and say, with
the man in the Gospel, ' I believe : help thou
mine unbelief.' "

Religious thoughts, however, did not
always calm her real disquietude and real
griefs. The religious and political situation
of England became daily more and more
gloomy, and Lady Russell, whose strongest

feelings were concerned, was daily more and more saddened and alarmed for her children, for her country, and for the prospects of the cause for which Lord Russell had laid down his life. The following extracts from her letters show her state of feeling at this time:

"Those are happy who, in the midst of confusions, can faithfully believe the end of all shall be rest; and if we can evidence to our hearts we have a title according to the promises of the gospel to that happy rest, what can be a very uneasy disturbance? Nothing should be, I am certain, yet we find pretences for it. I think I fear not myself, but I am afraid what risk my children may run; and if that were not, our weak faith would furnish us out with some other reason to justify, as we fancy, our too great carefulness. I will do what I can not to exceed, and so bid you adieu for this time."

"We in the country are still kept under wonder and expectation; the cloud is very thick that is spread over us; but this is our support (if we can but maintain our courage for a while), that nothing that can befall us can hurt us much; being the power of man reaches no farther than these frail bodies, that must, however, in a little while lie down, until that glorious day of the Lord, when all men's works shall be tried by a right judgment; then shall we see many justified that have stood condemned with the world: till then I desire to wait with patience."

"There is no time so hazardous but the righteous and the repentant may run unto God and be safe; and if we must not escape the judgments of the sword, yet I trust it shall cut off only such as most notoriously cumber God's ground; and that in the midst of wrath He will remember mercy, if we will

but meet Him in His judgments, as miserable
sinners ought to do; and as I question not
but numbers in this land do."

The revolution of 1688 put an end to this
position of pain and monotony. After five
years of mourning and depression, Lady
Russell suddenly saw her husband's cause
triumphant.

She was at Woburn during the two
months which elapsed between the landing
of the Prince of Orange in England and the
final departure of James. Far from London,
alone with her father-in-law and her children,
she yet was well-informed of what was
passing, and she watched the course of
events with the restrained interest of a
reasonable mind which knows the uncertainty
attending great designs, and with a religious
trust which leaves its family and country in
the hands of God. We see by her letters
that she diligently read the gazettes and

papers published on both sides, and that details of Town and Court news reached her frequently. Anxious for information, when she heard that Burnet had arrived with the Prince at Salisbury, she sent to him a letter by a special messenger.

"Curiosity," she says, "may be too eager, and therefore not to be justified, but sure it is unavoidable. I do not ask you should satisfy any part of it further than you can do in six lines. But I would see something of your handwriting upon English ground, and not read in print only the labour of your brains."

When the conflict approached its close, she went with the Earl of Bedford to pass some days in London, and it was probably then that, King James having requested Lord Bedford's assistance, the Earl said, "Sire, I had a son who might to-day have supported Your Majesty." Lady Russell had a near view of the scenes amid which William was seated on the throne.

"Those who have lived longest," she wrote to Dr. Fitzwilliam, "and therefore seen the most change, can scarce believe it is more than a dream : yet it is indeed real, and so amazing a reality of mercy as ought to melt and ravish our hearts into subjection and resignation to Him who is the dispenser of all providences."

Writing to Tillotson some time afterwards, she says : "The many public and signal mercies we have of late received are so reviving, notwithstanding the black and dismal scenes which are constantly before one, and particularly in these sad months, I must feel the compassions of a wise and good God to these late sinking nations, and to the Protestant interest all the world over, and all good people also. I raise my spirit all I can and labour to rejoice in the prospect of more happy days for the time to come than some ages have been blessed with. The goodness of those instruments God has called forth to work this great work by swells one's hopes."

Though she had kept up no regular communication with the Prince of Orange, they were not unknown or indifferent to each other. Letters occasionally passed between her and the Princess; and William knew too well the weight of Lord Russell's name in England, and the consideration in which his widow was held, not to pay her an especial regard. When he sent Dykevelt as Ambassador to England in 1687, he instructed him to visit Lady Russell, and in his name to express the deep esteem and great interest which he felt for her. Lady Russell, on the 24th of March 1687, gives an account of this visit, in which the Ambassador conveyed the Prince's expressions of good-will towards

her and the families with which she was
connected, and assurances that any request
she might make should be acceded to, adding
that he acted not as an individual, but as a
public minister. He repeated an expression
made use of by Mr. Skelton, the English
Ambassador at the Hague, when the news of
Lord Russell's death was received, to the
effect that the King had taken the life of one
man, but it would cost him perhaps several
thousand men.

CHAPTER IX

WILLIAM, when proclaimed King, did not delay publicly to confirm the language which his Minister had addressed to Lady Russell nearly two years before. On the evening of the 13th of February 1689, King William and Queen Mary—having in the morning accepted the Crown from Parliament—held their first public reception at Whitehall. Lady Russell was not there. Indisposed for all earthly pomp, even when her own cause was concerned, she quitted neither her house nor her mourning. Her daughter, Lady Cavendish, however, attended the Court with her mother-in-law, the Countess of Devonshire. Writing to a friend, she says: "At

night I went to Court with my Lady
Devonshire, and kissed the Queen's hand
and the King's also. There was a world of
bonfires, and candles almost in every house,
which looked extremely pretty. The King
applies himself mightily to business, and is
wonderfully admired for his great wisdom
and prudence in ordering all things. He is
a man of no presence, but looks very homely
at first sight; but if one looks long on him,
he has something in his face both wise and
good. But as for the Queen, she is really
altogether very handsome; her face is very
agreeable, and her shape and motions
extremely graceful and fine. She is tall, but
not so tall as the last Queen. Her room
was mighty full of company, as you may
guess."

Political action soon succeeded royal
civility. An Act was passed by Parliament
reversing the sentence on Lord Russell,

which it designated as murder. It was brought into the House of Commons "at the request of the Earl of Bedford and Lady Russell." Sir Thomas Clarges moved that these words should be omitted, because, said he, "national justice is above personal solicitation; this Act is not passed as a personal favour: all England is concerned in it." It was the second Act which received the royal assent after William's accession. A short time afterwards, to show favour at the same time to two families united by domestic ties as well as by political feelings, he raised the Earls of Bedford and Devonshire to the Dukedom. The letters patent of the new Duke of Bedford stated, among the grounds for this favour, "that this was not the least, that he was father to the Lord Russell, the ornament of his age, whose great merits 'twas not enough to transmit by history to posterity, but they were willing to record them in their royal patent, to remain in the family as a monument consecrated to his consummate virtue, whose fame would never be forgot so long as men preserved any esteem for sanctity of manner, goodness of mind, and a love of their country constant even to death. Therefore, to solace his excellent father for so great a loss, to celebrate the memory of so noble a son, and to excite his worthy grandson, the heir of such mighty hopes, more cheerfully to emulate and follow the example of his illustrious father, they entailed this high dignity upon the Earl and his posterity."

Family gratifications came to Lady Russell along with political restorations and honour. Her second daughter, Catherine, was married to Lord Roos, the eldest son of the Earl of Rutland; and her son to Miss Howland, a rich heiress of Surrey. In neither case did she decide hastily, or on mere considerations

of rank or fortune. On account of a divorce
which gave rise to some scruples, she
hesitated for some time before she allowed
her daughter to enter the family of the Earl
of Rutland, and she had refused a still more
wealthy alliance for her son. The brilliancy
of these marriages and the prosperity of the
family drew upon her the attention of all,
without any one being surprised or envious.
The public openly sympathised with this
reparation of injustice ; and the relations and
friends of the Russells, the Cavendishes, and
the Wriothesleys, took pleasure in reporting to Lady Russell in her retirement at
Southampton House the splendour of the
festivals in which she had no part. Her
daughter Catherine, after her marriage with
Lord Roos, was conducted by her husband
to Belvoir, the seat of the Earl of Rutland,
her father-in-law. On this occasion Sir James
Forbes—by whom, ten years previously,

Lord Cavendish had conveyed to Lord Russell the proposal to take his place in prison while he escaped—wrote to Lady Russell :

" MADAM,—I could not miss this opportunity of giving your Ladyship some account of Lord Roos and Lady Roos' journey, and their reception at Belvoir, which looked more like the progress of a King and Queen through their country, than that of a bride and bridegroom's going home to their father's house. At their first entry into Leicestershire, they were received by the High Sheriff at the head of all the gentlemen of the country, who all paid their respects to the lady bride at Harborough. She was attended next day to this place by the same gentlemen, and by thousands of other people, who came from all places of the country to see her, and to wish them both joy, even with huzzas and acclamations.

"As they drew near to Belvoir, our train increased, with some coaches and with fresh troops of aldermen, and corporations, besides a great many clergymen, who presented the bride and bridegroom with verses upon their happy marriage.

" I cannot better represent their first arrival at Belvoir, than by the Woburn song that Lord Bedford liked so well ; for at the gate were four-and-twenty fiddlers all in a row ; four-and-twenty trumpeters, with their tan-tara-ra-ra's ; four-and-twenty ladies, and as many parsons ; and in great order they went in procession to the great apartment, where the usual ceremony of saluting and wishing of joy passed, but still not without something represented in the song as very much tittle-tattle and fiddle-faddle. After this the time passed away till supper in visiting all the apartments of the house, and in seeing the preparations for the sack-posset, which was

the most extraordinary thing I did ever see,
and much greater than it was represented to
be.   After supper, which was exceedingly
magnificent, the whole company went in procession to the great hall: the bride and
bridegroom first, and all the rest in order,
two and two. There it was the scene opened,
and the great cistern appeared, and the
healths began,—first in spoons, some time
after in silver cups,—and though the healths
were many, and great variety of names
given to them, it was observed after one
hour's hot service, the posset did not sink
above one inch, which made my lady Rutland call in all the family, and then upon
their knees the bride and bridegroom's
health, with prosperity and happiness, was
drunk in tankards brim-full of sack-posset.
This lasted till past 12 o'clock.—Madam,
Your most humble and faithful servant,

1693.   " J. FORBES."

In addition to the account of these rejoic-
ings, Lady Russell received from some of her
friends congratulations which were doubtless
more in accordance with her own feelings.
Burnet writes : " I do heartily congratulate
with your Ladyship for this new blessing.
God has now heard your prayers with
relation to two of your children, which is a
good earnest that He will hear them in due
time with relation to the third. You begin
to see your children's children : God grant
you may likewise see peace upon Israel.
And now that God has so built up your
house, I hope you will set yourself to build
a house of prayer for the honour of His
name.

" You have passed through very different
scenes of life : God has reserved the best to
the last. I do make it a standing part of
my poor prayers twice a day, that as now
your family is the greatest in its three

branches that has been in England in our age, so that it may in every one of these answer those blessings by an exemplary holiness, and that both you and they may be public blessings to the age and nation."

She had only just married her son when she received a proposal respecting him equally singular and flattering. A General Election was at hand. The Duke of Shrewsbury, Lord Steward, and Lord Somers, Keeper of the Seals, caused a request to be conveyed to Lady Russell that she would agree to her son, notwithstanding his youth (he was only fifteen years of age), becoming a candidate for the County of Middlesex. "I made all the objections," says Sir James Forbes, "against it that I think the Duke of Bedford or your Ladyship can make, yet they were still of one opinion, that it is your interest, and for the honour of the family, that he should stand at present; and being joined with Sir John Worsename, a very honest man who is recommended by my Lord Keeper, they doubt not but they will carry it with a high hand, and thereby keep out two notorious Tories, which can never be done otherwise. When I told their Lordships that my Lord Tavistock was soon going to Cambridge, and afterwards to travel for two or three years, the Duke of Shrewsbury answered that they would not hinder anything of that design; for he needed not to appear but once at the election, when he would be attended by several thousands of gentlemen and other persons on horseback out of town, and the charges would be little or nothing; and the Duke of Shrewsbury bid me tell your Ladyship, that if you did consent he should stand, which he doubted not but you would, since it was on so good an account, that then they must have leave to set him up for that day only by the name of Lord Russell, which would bring ten thousand more on his side, if there be so many free-holders in the County."

Lady Russell had now received the utmost consolation the world could afford. Her husband's sentence had been reversed by the highest authority in the realm ; his cause had triumphed over all opposition ; and his family had received the highest honours. All that could gratify conjugal and maternal love and pride had been heaped upon her. These honours, however, did not remove her sense of the loss she had sustained ; nor did it disturb the sound-ness of her judgment. With respect to the honours bestowed on the Russell and Cavendish families, she says : " For the late circumstances in relation to the family, I would have assisted to my power for the procuring thereof ; but for any sensible joy at these outward things, I feel none." She prudently resolved to reject the premature political triumph offered to her son. In forwarding the letter containing the proposal for his election to her brother-in-law, Lord Edward Russell, with a request that he would see the Duke of Shrewsbury on the subject, she expresses her own and Lord Bedford's strong objections to it, and their conviction that the interruption of her son's studies would be fatal to his career.

Maternal discretion prevailed over party interests, and, instead of presenting himself to the electors of Middlesex, Lord Tavistock went to complete his education at the University, "where our young nobility," she wrote to Dr. Fitzwilliam, "should pass some of their time : it has been for many years neglected." She brought into the most ordinary incidents of private life the same sound judgment, the same uprightness and moral feeling, preserved thereby from the prejudices, the pride, and the frivolity which were too common among the old aristocracy. Before deciding to give her daughter Catherine to the son of the Earl of Rutland, she asked the latter whether his Lordship did not think it due to the young couple that they should see of each other a little more than they had done, and so at least guess at each other's humour, before they ventured to make them, as she hoped they would be, a happy couple. A few years later she had to dispose of the patronage of two livings. She wrote to one of her friends, Sir Robert Worsley: "I find both places well disposed to receive Mr. Swayne. I hope he is worthy of the gift, and believe you think him so. If you should know anything why he is not, though as a friend you might wish he were the incumbent, yet I am persuaded that in a just regard to the weight of the matter, and to me who ask it from you, if you know any visible reason that he is not a proper person for such a preferment, that you will caution me in it; for, I profess to you, Sir, I think the care of so many souls is a weighty charge, and I have been willing to take time to consider whose hands I put these into. I can, with all my scruples, make no exception to Mr. Swayne, if his vapours are not too prevalent to permit his being free and active in such a charge."

This union of virtue and good sense, the same throughout circumstances of the most varying character, amid the favours of fortune as well as under its reverses, acquired to Lady Russell among the people, as well as at the Court of England, a consideration and a moral influence such as few women have ever possessed. After their elevation to the Throne, King William and Queen Mary continued to show her the same respect as before, and paid the same attention to her wishes. At the time of the Revolution, when the formal consent of the Princess Anne to the coronation of the Prince of Orange was required, Lady Churchill, afterwards Duchess of Marlborough and confidant of the Princess, would not advise her to give it until she had consulted persons of undoubted integrity and wisdom, "especially Lady Russell and Dr. Tillotson." Tillotson himself long hesitated before he yielded to William's urgent desire that he should become Archbishop of Canterbury, fearing that the non-recognition of the King's title by a part of the clergy would interfere with his usefulness if he accepted the office from him. It was Lady Russell who decided him to yield. Consulted by him and informed of the pressure put upon him by the King, she wrote, after discussing and arguing against the Dean's scruples :

"The time seems to be come that you must put anew in practice that submission you have so powerfully both tried yourself and instructed others to. I see no place to escape at; you must take up the cross and bear it. I faithfully believe it has the figure of a very heavy one to you, though not from the cares of it; since, if the King guesses right, you toil more now; but this work is of your own choosing, and the dignity of the other is what you have bent your mind against, and the strong resolve of your life has been to avoid it. Had this even proceeded to a vow, it is, I think, like the virgin's of old, to be dissolved by the father of your country. Again, though contemplation, and a few friends well chosen, would be your grateful choice, yet if charity, obedience, and necessity call you into the great world, and where enemies encompass round about, must not you accept it? And each of these, in my mean apprehension, determines you to do it. In short, it will be a noble sacrifice you will make, and I am confident you will find as a reward kind and tender supports if you do take the burden upon you : there is, as it were, a commanding Providence in the manner of it. Perhaps I do as sincerely wish your thoughts at ease as any friend you have, but I think you may purchase that too dear ; and if you should come to think so too, they would then be as restless as before.

"Sir, I believe you would be as much a common good as you can ; consider how few of ability and integrity this age produces. Pray, do not turn this matter too much in your head ; when one has once turned it every way, you know that more does but perplex, and one never sees the clearer for it. Be not stiff, if it be still urged to you. Conform to the Divine Will, which has set it so strongly into the other's mind, and be

content to endure; it is God calls you to it.
I believe it was wisely said, that when there
is no remedy they will give it over and
make the best of it, and so I hope no ill will
terminate on the King; and they will lay up
their arrows when they perceive they are
shot in vain at him or you, upon whom no
reflection that I can think of can be made
that is ingenious; and what is pure malice,
you are above being affected with."

With her best friend, Dr. Fitzwilliam, she
had not the same success. She could not
overcome his scruples at taking the oath of
allegiance to William, and he left his living.
Lady Russell's attempt to dissuade him from
this course shows a conscientiousness equal
to his own. "I am very sorry," she writes,
"the case stands with you as it does in reference to the oath; and still wonder (unless I
could find Kings of divine right) why it does
so! And all this is the acceptation of a word

which I never heard two declare the meaning
of but they differed in their sense of it. You
say you could have taken it in the sense
some worthy men have done. Why will
you be more worthy than those men? It is
supererogation.

"If you can avoid mental reservation,
that's the biggest thing to me, for I hate
that to God or man; properly I know we
can have none to God, though we may wish
to have it; but I abhor that wish. But you
seem to say, though you are permitted to
declare, that is not enough, as not being
consistent with the simplicity of an oath,
and that it ought to be taken according to
the mind of the imposers. If you can take
it as those you mention have done, declaring
they meant legal obedience and peaceable
submission, I dare say you do so; no more
is meant to be imposed, especially by the
King and Queen. And does not being

content with the construction your friends
put upon it signify their permission to take
it in such a sense? It was my Lord Notting-
ham's misfortune to pitch upon that word
which gives such scruples. But methinks
(with submission to wiser heads) it should be
a greater to weaken the interest of the Church
and the Protestant religion all the world over
to the degree so many able men incapacitating
themselves to serve in the Church will do, if
God in much mercy prevent it not.

"It is above great and good men to
regard reflections, if they give not a just
cause of scandal: and in serving the cause
of God the best we can, there is none given.
It may very well be passive obedience went
too high. Some drove Jehu-like. If it
appears they perceive they did so, ought
there to be shame in that, or ought it not
to be borne cheerfully? If their nakedness
is laid open and some Hams do insult, still

they should be above it, and overcome evil
with good. I never thought good men had
any harm by the ill-natured speeches of
malicious spirits. God knows the very best
of men have infirmities, but they are ill men
that retort them. However, after all is said,
or can be said, a man must be quiet in his
own breast if he can. When I began to
write in this paper, I meant not one word
of all I have said on this subject; but I
know, good Doctor, you will take it right;
accept well of my good meaning towards
you, and excuse my defects. I pretend not
to argue, but where my wishes are earnest
I speak without reserve, sometimes by surprise; but take it as it is, I will not look
back to examine; I know I need not to you."

The difference made no change in their
friendship, and he requested her to take
charge of his library until he had deter-
mined upon his course.

CHAPTER X

ON all occasions Lady Russell, after the success of the cause in which she felt such deep interest, and amid the exaltation of her family, shows calm judgment and a liberality of mind and heart far removed from all inflated feeling, even as she had shown firmness and constancy under her trials. The following letters indicate the consideration for others with which she acted in business matters. The first is addressed to Sir Jonathan Trelawney, Bishop of Exeter, one of the seven bishops who were sent to the Tower in 1688.—

" MY LORD,—I am much obliged to your Lordship for the account you give me of

your transactions with Mr. Reinolds and
the Vicar of Tavistock, esteeming the pains
you have taken in being so particular both
as a respect and as proceeding from the
same motive that inclined me to speak with
your Chancellor, which was that this matter
might be amicably composed.   The late
Duke of Bedford was a person of great
justice, moderation, and courtesy, from which,
if he ever swerved, I dare say it was only
through misinformation ; but in managing
his business he was regular in his method,
doing it all generally by his officers, and
very reserved to his friends and relations.
I never knew anything of this difference till
some time after his Grace's death, that Mr.
Reinolds, his chief steward, applying himself
to me, among other things acquainted me
therewith, which he did upon occasion of a
letter he had lately received from the Vicar,
wherein he gave him to understand that

your Lordship had renewed your prosecution, and that he was under some apprehension that my son would not support him as his grandfather would have done; to which, out of pity to the grief and fear he expressed, I ordered the steward to reply to this effect: That my son being at Newmarket, he could give him at present no answer from him; but I bid him tell him from me that I did not doubt but my son would assist him in all things that were just and reasonable; and, resolving to get a relation of it as soon as I could from your Lordship's side, I found means to discourse with Doctor Edisbury, your Chancellor, of which, I suppose, he has given you a better account than I can. Had I not observed that most of the differences that are arise from not having patience, or not using proper means to be truly informed, I should have thought you had singled out this man; but by the course

I took I soon understood your orders were general. I agree, my Lord, the Vicar ought to observe the rubric, and obey all your canonical injunctions. I am sensible what good effect singing psalms musically has had in several parishes; and I am sorry a man, especially in so populous a place, should need to be ordered to read prayers Wednesdays and Fridays. In short, my Lord, neither I nor any that I can persuade will assist in opposing your just authority; and, saving that we are not of their mind who would lay pains and penalties upon people for not conforming to its worship, we are, as much as any, for supporting the Church of England, and encouraging communion with it.

"I am satisfied, my Lord, there are many would be very inconsiderable, were it not for being fierce of a party, and for that end they keep up a dissension, when the reason of it is ceased; but I wish those whom I am concerned for to value men according to their worth, and not for being of a party, and to be assured irreligious and immoral men, of whatever party they are, or whatever they profess, can never be true to friend or country, wanting the principle that should make them so. It highly imports my son to inquire into the things your Lordship relates of an officer of his; and if what he writ to one of the gentlemen you mention be extant, and were put into my son's hands, it would be an undeniable proof, and put the matter past all out-facing. I cannot conclude before I give your lordship my thanks for your obliging letters, and your favour to the Vicar, upon our account. My son will order his steward to advise him to be more observant for the future, and to let him know he must expect no countenance from him if he be irregular."

The following is taken from a letter to her cousin, the Earl of Galway:

"I am thankful to God I have made an end between Mr. Sp—— and myself. Now as I am to answer for Mr. Sp——, who was an accountant to me, being employed by me so, there is this article between him and me, that if any time there is a discovery of any money or debt due to him, I have the title to it, and not he, let it be much or little.

"After many offers and endeavours, by council and without, I came to this agreement: He was to make a clear and full· discovery of all he is worth—lands, leases, monies, goods, debts, etc. Then I, who was to have the whole in me, allow back to him what I think will be a subsistence to him, his wife and children. And so I have done. Swearing is what I desire to excuse; for it is possible he might be tempted to proceed in doing ill, and I not the better; and if he had sworn truth, as others professed they would not believe him, though I am less free in the professing of it, I might have doubted; then why provoke him to sin?

"What has been urged to me over and over again many times has no force in it, which was, that they would undertake, and are sure, he could conceal ten thousand pounds, which I should never discover, either in this nation or India. My answer is, if it cannot ever be found, it is to me as if it were not. And if I had any opinion of a conjuror (as we call them), I would not seek it that way. So what I approved best of, I chose.

"That if a discovery be made out it is to my use. Now, the farm he has from his father, which is £55 a year, I could not come at, all counsel agreeing it to be out of the way; nay, I must have had application to Chancery to have proceeded; there he could have hung it up. Sir Joseph Jekyll said this, that there it might hang for a dozen of years, nay, to the end of the youngest in the room, and Tom Selwood was one of the seven or eight: there were four counsel. Also, he said, he would not take five thousand pounds of me towards the charge I should be at. But all this avails not at all; nothing but prison, nay, dying on a dunghill has no ill sound. At last I gave no further trouble (after having endured so much myself), from the opinion of a great lawyer, though not now to be paid as counsel. After two hours' discourse, and laying all before him, he told me it was the most advisable thing to compound the matter; and he esteemed it a very good composition, where they pretended to seven or eight thousand pounds from me, to pay me between two and three. He was so vehement in his opinion of making an end, that as a friend he prayed and exhorted me to set to it next morning; and if it were his case he would not sleep till it was done, if that were possible, for if he should happen to die, I could not imagine how bad my circumstances might be, even to the returning two thousand pounds I had then received, and never be able to disprove his account, so be a debtor eight thousand pounds to his wife and children. This has given me many terrible waking hours from week to week, seeking to please and accommodate to my wishes; but they were not inclined to believe what they did not like; so took no impression, as I would think they did not believe it did on me; but I was no hypocrite; I felt more than I told, my mind is more at rest as to all my worldly concerns."

Once only she seems rather exacting.

She had strongly recommended for admission to the King's Council a distinguished young man, William Cowper, who afterwards, under George I., became Chancellor and Lord Cowper. Some strong objections were made to granting this request; a dispensation as to age was requisite. Lady Russell persisted, first to Lord Halifax, and afterwards to Sir H. Polloxfen, Attorney-General, her letter to whom concluded thus: "I undertake very few things, and therefore do very little good to people: but I do not love to be baulked, when I thought my end compassed: and though you would not promote us in it, I hope you will not destroy us." This is the only trace in all her correspondence of any departure from that reserve and consideration for others which marked her conduct. The claim was indeed authorised by the merit of him in whose behalf it was made; but the manner in which it was pressed seems to show an impatience at opposition which is not manifested in any other instance.

Her own sufferings taught her to sympathise with those who suffered the loss of friends. In 1690 her cousin M. de Ruvigny was killed at the battle of the Boyne, and Lady Russell wrote to his mother:

"Dieu nous a frappée, ma chère Madame, d'un coup qui nous paraît fort rude; mais Dieu ne pense pas comme l'homme pense, et il faut croire qu'il ne prend pas plaisir à tourmenter ses pauvres créatures. Mais que songeons-nous, que Dieu voulut se détourner de son chemin en ses providences pour notre contentement? Non, assurement: il faut nous supporter le mieux que nous puissions sur toutes sorte d'événements, et vivre en espérance qu'un jour nous verrons plus clairement la raison de tous ses noirs dispensations qui nous attaquent, qui nous touchent si vivement.

"Madame, je ne combats pas votre vive douleur, vous le devoyez, à un fils, et à un homme si brave et si amié ôté du monde.

"Il a aussi toutes sortes de consolations qu'on peut possible atteindre en la manière de sa mort ; en toutes ses dernières actions, mon âme me fait fort espérer qu'il fut accepté, et que son âme se repose en le bras de cet Sauveur en qui il se reposoit avec tant de foy.　Dieu veut, Madame, que vous et moy faisons nos devoirs en telle sorte que les accidents qui nous peuvent arriver ne nous détournent pas des sentiers de Dieu : mais au contraire nous ayant à passer douce-ment les peu de jours qui nous restent devant que nous entrons dans ces délices éternelles qu'il nous prépare."

Twenty-six years afterwards she wrote to his brother, Lord Galway, who, like herself,

had been called to mourn for his dearest connections : "I pray God to fortify your spirit
under every trial, till eternity swallows all
our troubles, all our sorrows, all our disappointments, and all our pains in this life. The
longest how short to eternity! All these
ought to be my own care to improve my
weak self, as the fortitude of your mind,
experience, and knowledge does to you.
And I pray for such a portion of them in
mercy to me as may secure an endless
glorifying to so feeble, so ignorant, so mean
a creature as myself, that I cannot be too
little in my own sight."

The following was addressed to Lady
Essex—the occasion does not appear :

"In what I can serve the just end you aim
at, I will be very diligent. And I beseech
God one day to speak peace to our afflicted
minds, and let us not be disappointed of our
great hope. But we must wait for our day of

consolation till this world passes away : an
unkind and trustless world it has been to us.
Why it has been such, God knows best : all
His dispensations serve the end of His providences ; and they are ever beautiful, and
must be good, and good to every one of us ;
and even these dismal ones are to us, if we
can bear evidence to our own souls, that we
are better for our afflictions ; which God
often makes them to be, who suffer wrong-
fully.   We   may   reasonably   believe   our
friends find that rest we yet but hope for ;
and what better comfort can your Ladyship
or I desire in this valley of the shadow of
death we are walking through ? The rougher
our path is, the more delightful and ravishing will the great change be to us."

In 1690 she lost her half-sister Lady
Montagu, and her nephew Lord Gainsborough. The following letters were written
on this occasion : the first to Tillotson ; the

others to Dr. Fitzwilliam and Bishop Burnet.—

" Your letters will never trouble me, Mr. Dean ; on the contrary, they are comfortable refreshments to my, for the most part, over-burthened mind, which both by nature and by accident is made so weak that I cannot bear with that constancy I should the losses I have lately felt. I can say, Friends and acquaintances Thou hast hid out of my sight, but I hope it shall not disturb my peace. These were young, and as they had begun their race of life after me, so I desired they might have ended it also. But happy are those whom God retires in His grace—I trust these were so ; and then no age can be amiss : to the young it is not too early, nor to the aged too late. Submission and prayer is all we know that we can do towards our own relief in our distress, or to disarm God's anger, either in our public or our private concerns. The scene will soon alter to that peaceful and eternal home in prospect. But in this time of our pilgrimage vicissitudes of all sorts are every one's lot."

"There is so much in those little sheets you sent me to thank you for, that, finding myself very ill-fitted to do it, I was tempted to let it quite alone, till I made shift to consider that, for the most part, our temptations incline us to the worst things, and to the most forbidden tempers. This makes me rise from that listlessness I continually drop into till I have at least told you how sensible I am of your kindness on all occasions; and I am sensible too how strong and pious all your offers of comfort to a disquieted mind are, and I hope that by often perusing them they will so affect me that the effect shall correspond to your Christian wishes and prayers for me, and I

shall obtain a better freedom of mind than
I am mistress of at present, since you
conjecture very truly, every new stroke to a
weary, battered carcass makes me struggle
the harder; and though I lost with my best
friend all the delights of living, yet I find I
did not want a quick sense of new grief for
want of due considering that whatever below
God is the object of our love will, at some
time or other, be the matter of our sorrow.
These two, my sister and a dear sister's son,
began their course after me, but have ended
it sooner. I would have had it otherwise,
but I was vain and foolish in it. God knows
where it is best to place His creatures. Your
prayers are indeed of more use than your
fears, for my health is good; but I love greatly
the prayers of my friends, that I may be re-
signed in the case of my children; for this trial
has so experienced to me my sad weakness
that I doubt myself, and humbly beg in mercy,

but not in judgment, that I may be spared that trial." ————

"I have, my Lord, so upright an heart to my friends that though your great weight of business had forced you to a silence of this kind, yet I should have had no doubt but that one I so distinguished in that little number God has yet left me does join with me to lament my late losses. The one was a just sincere man, and the only son of a sister and a friend I loved with too much passion ; the other, my last sister, and I ever loved her tenderly.

"It pleases me to think that she deserves to be remembered by all those that knew her. But after above forty years' acquaintance with so amiable a creature, one must needs, in reflecting, bring to remembrance so many engaging endearments as are yet at present embittering and painful ; and indeed we may be sure that when anything below

God is the object of our love, at one time or another it will be a matter of our sorrow. But a little time will put me again into my settled state of mourning; for a mourner I must be all my days upon earth, and there is no need I should be other; my glass runs low; the world does not want me, nor I want that; my business is at home, and within a narrow compass. I must not deny, as there was something so glorious in the object of my biggest sorrow, I believe that in some measure kept me from being then overwhelmed. So now it affords me, together with the remembrance how many easy years we lived together, thoughts that are joy enough for one who looks no higher than a quiet submission to her lot, and such pleasures in educating the young folks as surmounts the cares that it will afford. If I shall be spared the trial, where I have most thought of being prepared to bear the pain, I hope I

shall be thankful, and I think I ask it faithfully, that it may be in mercy, not in judgment. Let me rather be tortured here, than
they or I be rejected in that other blessed
peaceful home to all ages to which my soul
aspires. There is something in the younger
going before me that I have observed all
my life to give a sense I cannot describe;
it is harder to be borne than a bigger loss,
where there has been spun out a longer
thread of life. Yet I see no cause for it,
for every day we see the young fall with the
old, but methinks it is a violence upon nature.

"A troubled mind has a multitude of
these thoughts. Yet I hope I master all
murmurings; if I have had any, I am sorry,
and will have no more, assisted by God's
grace; and rest satisfied that, whatever I
think, I shall one day be entirely satisfied
what God has done and shall do will be
best, and justify both His justice and mercy."

CHAPTER XI

As she advanced in years, respected by all, satisfied in her family, and rejoicing in the prospects of her country, Lady Russell gradually changed. Without healing her wound, time, use, that self-renunciation which high-toned characters acquire with age, blunted the sharpness of the pain; the same remembrances, the same regrets, equally strong, had not the same power; her affection for her children, her solicitude for their conduct and their happiness, occupied more of her thoughts and left less room for retrospection; devotion, duty, became her habitual life. She was more calm and re-signed, more and more submissive to the

Divine will, looking forward to the coming eternity, and more occupied in preparing for it. These are the feelings manifested in a long letter which she wrote to her children, before the marriages of her son and of her younger daughter, in which she gave them, with the utmost freedom, the counsels, the exhortations, the example of her faith and love.

" My dear children," she says,—" I write this upon the 21st of July 1691—a day of sad remembrances to me, it being that whereon your excellent father was taken from us with much severity, to my lasting sorrow and your loss.

" I have not yet omitted on this day (but when prevented by sickness) to humble and afflict myself under the mighty hand of God, pouring out my soul before Him in prayer and fasting. As, first, to testify my humiliation for all my sins, for my having offended God

in so many and so frequent breaches of my
baptismal vow, my Sacrament vows, and
all those vows I have at any other time
made of a better and more strict obedience
to all His holy commandments, I recollect,
as well as I can, what they have been, and
make my resolutions to do better for the
time to come, and as a help to my memory,
I did now look over some notes I had by
me of some former examination; at other
times I have done it by considering all the
passages of my life which I have by me
noted in a paper after the same manner I
set yours down, and gave it you when you
first received the Sacrament."   She goes on
to describe the daily exercises to which she
had accustomed herself in order that none
of her actions should escape a scrupulous
examination, her habitual prayers, her read-
ings, whether in the Scriptures or in works
of religious instruction and edification.   "On

every Friday," she says, " I take my paper, and consider what I have been most faulty in this week—as wandering in prayer, or negligent in reading, or passionate, or envious, or what else. I set it down (in as few words as I can) at the foot of my daily notes for that week ; and so that is an abridgment for the whole week. Saturday morning begins the next week. And upon the first Friday in every month, or the last, just before I use my confession, I look upon my notes and consider the actions of the whole month—if nothing but common has happened, the less examination will suffice ; only I take care so to recollect as may represent anything that is remarkable or great, either to be matter of sorrow or thanksgiving (for other things a general care is proportionable), and make my resolutions accordingly ; and when I have done my devotions, I set down in a book I have to that purpose, at the weeks of that month, as I have made an abridgment of them, and then I tear my piece of paper and take a new one for the next month.

"This gets on a habit of constant watchfulness; and at Sacrament times, or at any other time that I would examine myself, I find it a great help to read this. It saves much time in looking back, and one's thoughts are less distracted, and makes our lives more easy to us, when we see how we live from one Sacrament to another. And this makes religion easy, and the mind quiet and full of tranquillity; and though it may seem a hard task at first, yet a little use makes it none, though if it be,—for flesh and blood is apt to draw back at the times of devotion, and especially at such-like exercise, —yet if it help us to live more innocently, and to state things more reverently and usefully between God and our souls, no pains is too much, but, on the contrary, doing this will upon trial (I speak it by experience) be found less pains to such as mean to be serious in religion and do desire to do their duty well and with cheerfulness: and is hugely more satisfying to the mind than a more careless, loose way of living is, and no settled method. . . . And now, my dear child, I have but little more to add, except to put you in mind to remember this life at longest is but short, and how short none can tell; but if you live, crosses will come, and pleasures wear away. Strive to get gospel evidence of your being a child of God, and having a title to the promises of eternal life. I call gospel evidence the being able to take my hopes of being saved by my sincere endeavours I use to live up to the rule of the Bible; therefore read it carefully all your life, learn some of it by heart, some I have named.

"It is this, believe me, my dear child, it

is the witness of an honest and good life in
the day of trouble and distress. No refreshment then but in a well-founded hope to
enjoy a happy eternity, and to what a degree
that calms and sweetens the most bitter
sorrows is inconceivable by such as have
not felt it, as I bless God I have ever since
I could get over the astonishment of so great
and so sudden a blow. When I am cast down
with some sad reflections [on] what I have
lost, I do as soon as I can sum my thoughts
to consider that in a short time I shall leave
this world and go to a place where I shall
see Him who died for me. I shall then know
much of the reason of all those providences
we do now so little understand, and think so
severe. I shall meet all my pious friends
again, and what a joy will it be to feel
continual springs of pleasure, a perpetual
and entire quiet in our own minds: no
sickness, no bad appetite, no passion shall

remain in us, but a constant joy in being extremely good; and that the sense that this will be perpetual must add a freshness to that fulness of joy which could not be entire if we did not foresee would be endless. O blessed, longed-for day! Yet I am willing to continue for your good (I think so). But if that care were over, it is very likely flesh and blood would find some other reason to be willing to continue. Nature shrinks at the separation of soul and body, and there is a love of living implanted in our natures; and how well is it that it is so, to help us to endure the crosses and the toils and labours of life. Yet I can think of this day of death with sweet refreshment, and 'tis pleasantness to my thoughts. O, my beloved children, take care we meet again; do but experience the pleasure of a well-spent life, and the pure delights of meditating on the future state of Eternity. That you may do so, and love it, to my last breath you will have the prayers of a truly loving mother. Consider, my dear, that all the innocent delights of life you may take and no anxiety of mind with it; but if they shut out religious thoughts and performances and devour and take up all our time, then indeed we sin, and conscience will sting at some time or other and be a sore remembrancer and check us in our gaiety; but be devout and regular in your duties to God—heaven will be secure, and pleasures innocent."

The following passages from her letters show the solicitude with which she watched over her children, and how wisely she advised them. About two years after the marriage of her younger daughter, she writes thus to her—the occasion does not appear:

" I must not be long, and therefore hasten to remind you of your former promises to strive to take every providence patiently

and as cheerfully as you can, and not foolishly
pine and waste your spirits and spoil your
health against a better day comes, which
certainly will, if you provoke not the only
Giver of all good things. Heaviness may
endure for a night, but joy cometh in the
morning ; and the chiefest blessing on this
earth you have, a kind husband and a pretty
gentleman. Let that sweeten all other
meaner things, as it is your duty it should
do. Strive to act your part and glory in it :
it is a pride I can allow of : but all discontent
proceeds from a pride that must be resisted,
or a poor mortal can never be happy on
earth, or prepared to be so in heaven. Can
we without imprudence say to Him that
made us, Why is it thus and thus with me ?
Ask yourself what have you done, or what
can man do, to merit from God ? Have not
you many good things others want that are
perhaps more humble than you, but still their

submission is not tried enough; but when it is, and they are as gold refined in the furnace, how greatly shall they be exalted for evermore, and respected here? Take it well, my love: I remind you of your duty, and let it be your part to strive to do it. To whom asks it shall be given. You shall be contented if you desire it; I have experienced it just at your years. I bless God I can say (without vanity) what pleased me I enjoyed, what crossed me had not power to torment me long. I strove to think if my lot had not been what it was it might have been worse for me in regard to my eternal interest, and that might pass and other days come, or however the day of vexation would end; and I cannot commend a better reflection than this, that troubles or pleasures that end with time are not to be affecting at too high a rate. A year or two to come seems long, but twenty past as nothing. I have felt

many days of bitter grief as well as others of
lesser trouble and provocation, and many of
great and true happiness which was made up
by love and quiet at home, abroad friendships
and innocent diversions; and yet, believe
me, child, life is a continual labour chequered
with care and pleasure; therefore rejoice in
your portion—take the world as you find it,
and you will, I trust, find that heaviness may
endure for a night but joy comes in the
morning. It grows dark; your sister is to
close this from [your] well-wishing Mother."

The following is from a letter to the Rev.
J. Thornton respecting her son :

" My constant prayer is, that his studies
may be innocent and profitable, that is (in
my thoughts), directed to his most spiritual,
his precious and immortal soul. I lie under
no discouragements, for yesterday Mr.
Hicks speaks of him to me when we are
alone just as he did. Logic goes forward

very well, and he says his judgment is wonderful nice and true; what he reads alone he gives a very handsome account of. He tried him the other day, by a new treatise on logic that the Dean of Christ Church has lately printed, but he observes he does not love to go over what he has once done. They have a Bible bound up with blank leaves, and in them, as he reads, he intends he shall write as he expounds any hard text."

Nine years afterwards Lady Russell writes to her son, who had meanwhile succeeded his grandfather as second Duke of Bedford:

"When I take my pen to write this, I am, by the goodness and mercy of God, in a moderate and easy state of health—a blessing I have thankfully felt through the course of a long life, which (with a much greater help) the contemplation of a durable state has maintained and upheld me through

varieties of providences and conditions of
life. But all the delights and sorrows of this
mixed state must end; and I feel the decays
that attend old age creep so fast on me[1]
that, although I may get over some more
years however, I ought to make it my
frequent meditation that the day is near
when this earthly tabernacle shall be dissolved and my immortal spirit be received
into that place of purity where no unclean
thing can enter, there to sing eternal praises
to the great Creator of all things. With the
Psalmist, I believe, 'at His right hand there
are pleasures for evermore'; and what is
good and of eternal duration must be joyful
above what we can conceive, as what is evil
and of like duration must be despairingly
miserable. And now, my dear child, I pray,
I beseech you, I conjure you, my loved son,
consider what there is of felicity in this world

[1] Lady Russell was now over seventy years of age.

that can compensate the hazard of losing an
everlasting easy being; and then deliberately
weigh whether or no the delights and gratifications of a vicious or idle course of life are
such that a wise or thoughtful man would
choose or submit to. Again, fancy its enjoyments at the height imagination can propose
or suggest, which yet rarely or never happens,
or, if it does, as a vapour, soon vanishes; but
let us grant it could, and last to fourscore
years, is this more than the quickest thought
to eternity? O my child, fix on that word
'eternity'! Old Hobbes, with all his fancied
strength of reason, could never endure to
rest or stay upon that thought, but ran from
it to some miserable amusement. I remember
to have read of some man, who, reading in
the Bible something that checked him, threw
it on the ground; the book fell open, and
his eye fixed on the word 'eternity,' which so
struck upon his mind that he from a bad liver

became a most holy man. Certainly nothing besides the belief of reward and punishment can make a man truly happy in his life, at his death, and after death. Keep innocency, and take heed to the thing that is right, for that shall bring a man peace at the last— peace in the evening of each day, peace in the day of death, and peace after death. For my own part, I apprehend I should not much care (if free from pain) what my portion in this world was—if a life to continue perhaps one year, or twenty, or eighty ;—but then to be dust, not to know or be known any more—this is a thought has something of horror in it for me, and always had, and would make me careless if it were to be long or short ; but to live, to die to live again, has a joy in it, and how inexpressible is that joy if we secure an humble hope to live ever happily ; and this we may do if we take care to live agreeably to our rational faculties, which also best secures health, strength, and peace of mind, the greatest blessings on earth. Believe the Word of God, the Holy Scriptures, the promises and threats contained in them; and what most obstructs our doing so, I am persuaded, is fear of punishment. Look up to the firmament, and down to the deep: how can any doubt a Divine power? And if there is, what can be impossible to infinite power? Then why an infidel in the world? And if not such, who then would hazard a future state for the pleasure of sin a few days? No wise man, and indeed no man that lives and would desire to see good days; for the laws of God are grateful. In His Gospel the terrors of majesty are laid aside and He speaks in the still and soft voice of His Son incarnate, the fountain and spring whence flows gladness. A gloomy and dejected countenance better becomes a galley slave

than a Christian, where joy, love, and hope
should dwell. The idolatrous heathen performed their worship with trouble and terror;
but a Christian and a good liver, with a
merry heart and lightsome spirit; for
examine and consider well, where is the
hardship of a virtuous life? When we have
moderated our irregular habits and passions
and subdued them to the obedience of reason
and religion, we are free to all the innocent
gratifications and delights of life; and we
may lawfully, nay, further, I say we ought
to, rejoice in this beautiful world, and all
the conveniences and provisions, even for
pleasure, we find in it; and which, in much
goodness, is afforded us to sweeten and allay
the labours and troubles incident to this
mortal state, nay, inseparable, I believe, by
disappointments, cross accidents, bad health,
unkind returns for good deeds, mistakes even
among friends, and, what is more touching,

death of friends. But in the worst of these calamities, the thought of a happy eternity does not alone support, but also revive, the spirit of man ; and he goeth forth to his labour with inward comfort, till the evening of his day (that is, his life on earth), and with the Psalmist cries out: 'I will consider thy heavens, even the works of thy fingers : the moon and the stars, which thou hast ordained. What is man, that thou art mindful of him : and the son of man, that thou shouldst so regard him ?' (Ps. viii.). 'Thou madest him lower than the angels: to crown him with glory.' Here is matter of praise and gladness. 'The fool,' as the Psalmist ex-presses it, 'hath said in his heart, there is no God.' Or let us consider the man who is content to own an invisible power, yet tries to believe that when man has done living on this earth he lives no more ; but I would ask if any of these unhappy creatures

are fully persuaded, or that there does not
remain in these men at times (as in sickness
or sober thoughtfulness) some suspicion or
doubt that it may be other than they try to
think. And although they may, to shun such
a thought, or be rid of such a contemplation, run away from it to some unprofitable
diversion, or perhaps suffer themselves to
be rallied out of such a thought, so de-
structive to the way they walk in; yet, to be
sure, that man does not feel the peace and
tranquillity he does who believes a future
state and is a good man. For although this
good man, when his mind may be clouded
with some calamity very grievous to him,
or the disorder of vapours to a melancholy
temper, I say, if he is tempted to some
suspicion that it is possible it may be other
than he believes (pray observe), such a
surmise or thought, nay, the belief, cannot
drive him to any horror; he fears no evil,

because he is a good man, and with his life all sorrow ends too; therefore it is not to be denied he is the wisest man who lives by the Scripture rule and endeavours to keep God's laws. First, his mind is in peace and tranquillity; he walks sure who keeps innocence and takes heed to the thing that is right. Secondly, he is secure God is his friend, that Infinite Being; and He has said, ' Come unto me, ye that are heavy laden; my yoke is easy '; but guilt is certainly a heavy load; it sinks and damps the spirits. ' A wounded spirit who can bear?' And the vile subtle spirit waits (I am persuaded) to drive the sinner to despair; but godliness makes a cheerful heart.

"Now, O Man, let not past errors discourage. Who lives and sins not? God will judge the obstinate, profane, unrelenting sinner, but full of compassion to the work of his own hand, if they will cease from

doing evil and learn to do well, pray for
grace to repent, and endeavour with that
measure which will be given, if sincerely
asked for, for at what time soever a sinner
repents (but observe, this is no license to
sin because at any time we may repent; for
that day we may not live to see, and so,
like the fool in the parable, our lamps be
untrimmed when we are called upon). Remember that to forsake vice is the beginning
of virtue; and virtue certainly is most con-
ducive to content of mind and a cheerful
spirit.   He (the virtuous man) rejoiceth with
a friend in the good things he enjoys; fears
not the reproaches of any; no evil spirit can
approach to hurt him here, or accuse him in
the great day of the Lord, when every soul
shall be judged according as they have done
good or evil.   O blessed state! fit for life,
fit for death!   In this good state I wish and
pray for all mankind; but most particularly,

and with all the ardour I am capable of, to those I have brought into the world and those dear to me. Thus are my fervent and frequent prayers directed that you may die the death of the righteous, and, to this end, that Almighty God would endue all with spiritual wisdom to discern what is pleasing in his sight."

CHAPTER XII

THUS did Lady Russell attempt to lead her children in the path in which she had found peace and consolation. It would be difficult to find a motherly exhortation so sweet and solemn, or in which anxious affection is manifested in close alliance with fervent piety. She had need to keep her faith in exercise: her trials were not yet over. Twenty years after she had addressed this letter to her children, she was at the bedside of her son, the Duke of Bedford, who had been suddenly attacked with smallpox; the young Duchess and her children had been sent away for fear of infection; the mother remained alone, receiving the last words, soothing the last moments of her dying son, and directing his thoughts heavenward. "Alas, my dear Lord Galway," she wrote to her cousin, "my thoughts are yet all disorder, confusion, and amazement, and I think I am very incapable of saying or doing what I should. I did not know the greatness of my love to his person, till I could see it no more. When nature, who will be mistress, has in some measure, with time, relieved herself, then, and not till then, I trust the Goodness which hath no bounds, and whose power is irresistible, will assist me by His grace to rest contented with what His unerring providence has appointed and permitted. And I shall feel ease in this contemplation, that there was nothing un-comfortable in his death but the losing him. His God was, I verily believe, ever in his thoughts. Towards his last hours he called upon Him, and complained he could not

pray his prayers. To what I answered, he
said he wished for more time to make up
his accounts with God. Then with remembrance to his sisters, and telling me how
good and kind his wife had been to him,
and that he should have been glad to have
expressed himself to her, said something to
me of my double kindness to his wife, and
so died away. There seemed no reluctancy
to leave this world, patient and easy the
whole time, and I believe knew his danger,
but, loth to grieve those by him, delayed
what he might have said. But why all this?
The decree is past. I do not ask your
prayers; I know you offer them with sincerity to our Almighty God for your afflicted
kinswoman."

Six months had scarcely elapsed when a
fresh blow fell. Her second daughter, the
Duchess of Rutland, died in childbirth. Of
her three children, her eldest daughter, the

Duchess of Devonshire, alone was left, and had also just been confined. In order to conceal from her her sister's death, Lady Russell said, in answer to her inquiry, "I have seen your sister out of bed to-day." She had seen her in her coffin.

Lady Russell knew herself better, and judged herself more severely, than the most rigid moralist could do. She was in the habit, as we have seen from her letter to her children, of constant and searching self-examination; and after her death an unfinished paper was found, written in a hand feeble with age, in which, in the form of a prayer, she took a review of her life, an account of her faults and her sins, and besought God's forgiveness for them. "Vanity cleaves to me, I fear, O Lord," she writes, "in all I say, in all I do. In all I suffer proud, not enduring to slights or neglects, subject to envy the good parts of others, even as to worldly gifts. Failing in my duty to my superiors; apt to be soon angry, with and without cause, too often; and by it may have grieved those that desired to please me, or provoked others to sin by my rash anger. Not ready to own any advantage I may have received by good advice or example. Not well satisfied if I have not all the respect I expected even from my superiors. Such has been the pride of my naughty heart, I fear, and also neglect in my performances due to my superiors, children, friends, or servants."

Her self-condemnation may appear excessive; but in thus accusing herself of pride and neglect of others, she shows that she was aware of her own defects, and was as penetrating as she was sincere.

About 1690 her sight began to fail, and the few letters which remain from her later years are short, chiefly on matters of business

or family concerns; they breathe an air of
calm sadness, like those of a captive who
had seen all those whom she loved escape
from their prison, and was awaiting her own
turn for deliverance. A successful operation
for cataract partially restored her sight; but
she frequently speaks of 'the necessity of
sparing her eyes. In September 1723 she
was alone at Southampton House, where
she had lived with her father, her husband,
and since her widowhood. On the 26th
her grand-daughter, Lady Rachel Morgan,
wrote to her brother, Lord James Cavendish:
" The bad account we have received of grandmamma Russell has put us into great disorder and hurry. Mamma has left us, and
gone to London. . . . I believe she has
stopped the letters on the road, for none
have come here to-day, so that we are still
in suspense. The last post brought us so
bad an account that we have reason to fear

the worst. I should be very glad that Mamma should get to town time enough to see her, because it might be some satisfaction to both, and I hear Grandmamma asked for her."

They were allowed this last consolation. Lady Russell died on the 29th, in the arms of her only remaining child. The *Weekly Journal* of October 5 announced her death thus: "The Right Honourable the Lady Russell, relict of Lord Russell, died on Sunday morning last, at five o'clock, at Southampton House, aged eighty-six, and her corpse is to be carried to Chenies, in Buckinghamshire, to be interred with that of her lord." A week later another journal chronicled the funeral. Thus, after her long and chequered life, the last words of Lord Russell to Burnet were fulfilled for his wife, as they had been for himself: she had done with time, she had entered eternity.

LADY HERBERT

In the romantic expedition made by Charles I. into Spain, when Prince of Wales, to see the Infanta Isabella, who had been proposed to him for a bride, he was accompanied, or followed, by some young Englishmen of rank, who were smitten, like their Prince, with the chivalrous spirit of the times. Among these the most eminent, next to the imperious favourite Buckingham himself, was Sir Edward Herbert (a kinsman of Lord Herbert of Cherbury, and of the sweet and pious poet of the same name), then a youth of three-and-twenty, distinguished equally by his personal and mental graces, excelling in all martial exercises, and uniting in his character that mixture of hardihood and gentleness which formed an accomplished cavalier.

Sir Walter Aston was then resident at the Spanish Court, under the Earl of Bristol, who had been sent on a special mission to negotiate the Royal Marriage. Sir Walter was related to the great Earl of Strafford, whose tragical end afterwards added a deeper shade to the fate of his unfortunate master. Sir Walter's eldest daughter, known in the phrase of that period as Mistress Amabel Aston, was esteemed the most charming woman of her time, and celebrated in masques and Court poems as the Rose of England. She then resided with her father at Madrid; and it may well be supposed that such a maid, then in the first bloom of youth and loveliness, would make a deep impression on the gay and gallant company who were assembled at the Court of Spain.

Even Prince Charles himself was struck, and it was whispered among the Court gossips that the beauty of the Infanta herself grew dim in his eyes, when compared with the charms of his fair country - woman. But Charles was a man of prudence and virtue. He saw that it would be improper to offer his hand to the daughter of a subject; and he would not urge his passion on other terms. Among all this noble assemblage, the person preferred by the fair Mabel was Sir Edward Herbert. Indeed, the merits and attractions of both were so conspicuous that they were at once destined for each other by the public voice. Charles approved of the union; and some time afterwards, on the return of Sir William's family to England, the Prince dignified the nuptials by his presence.

When Charles succeeded his father, Sir Edward and Lady Herbert were among the brightest ornaments of his Court, and continued to be distinguished by his favour. On the breaking out of troubles, they were zealous in the Royal cause. The good sense of Sir Edward disposed him to moderate counsels; but such was his habitual venera-tion for the King, and horror at what he deemed the unnatural disloyalty of his subjects, that he was prevented from exer-cising the native justness of his intellect, or urging measures that were distasteful to Charles. At length, all compromises having failed, resource was had to arms; the king-dom was delivered up to the miseries of civil war.

Sir Edward Herbert was now one of the most active and prudent of the King's adherents in battle, as he had formerly been in council. His estates lying in the western counties (where the disposition was always the most favourable to the Royal cause), he had the means of raising a considerable force among his friends and tenantry for the assistance of Charles.

The first movements in the field were rather to the advantage of the Royalists; but at the fatal battle of Edgehill they met with a complete discomfiture. In this engagement Sir Edward Herbert distinguished himself greatly; but no capacity or exertion could prevail against the evil fortunes of Charles.

Lady Herbert had continued to reside in London. She was now the mother of a large family—many of them very young, with whom it would have been difficult to follow the movements of the Royal army; while a residence at Sir Edward's country seat would have been full of danger (remote as it was, and without defence) in the distracted state of the country. Her situation in London, however, was neither pleasant nor safe. Among the sour fanatics who governed there, little delicacy was to be expected towards a woman, however lovely, or unfortunate; little toleration for an adherent of the Established Church; little favour for the wife of Sir Edward Herbert, and the kinswoman of Lord Strafford. Although her conduct was guarded by the strictest circumspection and her correspondence with her husband confined to the ordinary concerns of her house and family (a precaution the more needful that their letters were often intercepted), she was exposed to frequent disturbance from the wilder agitation of the time. She was even more than once summoned before a Committee of the Parliament "to stand question" (as it was termed) "touching the evil character of the Malignants." Her behaviour on such occasions was so strongly marked by dignity, gentleness, and discretion, that no grounds of complaint could be found against her; and the fierce nature of her inquisitors was almost softened to respect and pity.

As the civil war advanced, it became impossible for her to remain longer in London with any comfort or safety. She lived in daily fear of insult; and there was risk that she and her children might be detained as hostages for her husband. Therefore, she left London privately, with her family; and, escaping all interruption, joined Sir Edward, who was then with the King at Oxford. She continued to accompany the motions of the army—residing, with her family, at the nearest towns—till the fatal affair of Naseby, which scattered the King's party and brought ruin on his cause.

On the day of the decisive action, Lady Herbert was residing at the town of Northampton, which is several miles from the field of battle. Early in the engagement, reports arrived of the most favourable kind for the King's party, grounded on the successful charge of Prince Rupert. These were magnified by every tongue, and the King's adherents were full of joy and triumph and vengeance on the Roundheads. When these rumours reached Lady Herbert, she was in company with her kinsman old Sir Thomas Maynard, who had been wounded at the skirmish of Cropredy Bridge, and was still unable to take the field. When she asked his opinion of the news, he shook his head, and answered, "'Tis fit, fair cousin, we hope the best; but when I think of Marston Moor, I like not such passages." Then came varying rumours of good and evil. One bore that Cromwell was slain; the next, that the King was unhorsed and taken prisoner. At length the Royal troops were seen flying in scattered parties. Squadrons of the enemy's horse appeared in pursuit. It was too plain that the King's army had been overthrown.

To the anxious inquiries of Lady Herbert about the fate of her husband, the fugitives who reached the town of Northampton returned doubtful and contradictory answers. He had made himself so conspicuous in the action that there were many reports about him. It was said that he had fled with the King; that he had fallen in the field; that he was wounded and a prisoner. What confirmed Lady Herbert's fears was that on all former occasions of this kind her husband had contrived to send her private intelligence of his safety. Now the day passed over, and night approached, and she heard nothing. She was convinced that he had fallen in the field. He might be wounded and still recoverable. Whilst she endeavoured to appear cheerful, in order to soothe and pacify her children, she privately communicated her thoughts to Sir Thomas Maynard, and at the same time declared her resolution to go herself, that night, to the field and search for his body. "I beseech you, cousin," said he, "not to think of it. Let your faithful servant Travers go instead. Would I could go myself!" "Alas, no!" said Lady Herbert, "who will persevere like me?"—"Yet bethink you of the dangers which you run—the straggling parties, the lawless marauders, the spoilers of the slain."—"I were an unfit wife for Edward Herbert, an unworthy daughter of the house of Wentworth, could dangers stop me in such a cause. Yet, for precaution's sake, I will take Travers with me."

At midnight, after seeing her children put to rest, Lady Herbert rode towards the field of battle. She was attended by her servant

Travers, the son of one of Sir Edward's
tenants, and generally his close companion
in the field, but of late entrusted with the
still dearer charge of his wife and children.
This had been against her wishes, and she
could not forbear saying to him as they
rode: "Travers, hadst thou been with him,
methinks this would not have befallen. We
could have spared thee better than thy master
could." "Indeed, so please your ladyship,"
answered he, "it went hard that I could not
attend my honoured master in the battle:
I might have done him some service."
Travers led a third horse with a blanket
and some other necessaries, in case they
should find Sir Edward wounded. In this
state they reached the field of Naseby.

It was a chill and boisterous night, the
moon breaking out by fits between the
clouds which drove over the sky. As
they approached the field they met frequent

stragglers laden with spoil; and here and there lay a miserable wounded man imploring help which they could not give. When they reached the scene of action, all was silent. The living array and the throng of war had passed on, and nothing remained but the still and motionless heaps of the dead and dying. The moon sometimes gave a prospect over the encumbered field. Here the dead were piled closely together; there they had fallen dispersed in broken flight. Here was struck to earth the head grizzled by age; there the glossy ringlets of youth lay soiled in blood. Mangled limbs were scattered about, mixed with the carcasses of horses, gun-carriages, and broken tumbrils. Elsewhere were small-arms and fragments of feathers and clothing. The spoilers of the dead had now nearly done their work; but one or two straggling women still moved up and down like spectres among the heaps of slain. Lady Herbert had dismounted, and was picking her cautious and shuddering steps over the obstructed ground. She made up to one of the women, and asked if she could tell where the King's Guards had fought. "Aye, gossip," answered she. "Be'est thou come arifling too? But i' faith thou'rt of the latest. The swashing gallants were as fine as peacocks; but we've stript their bravery, I trow. Yonder stood the King's tent; and yonder about do most of them lie; but thou'lt scarce find a lading for thy cattle now."

Lady Herbert went, by this direction, towards a rising ground where the fragments of the royal tent were still to be seen. The dead here lay wedged in close heaps, indicating that the conflict had been long and desperate. The combatants had often fallen in mortal struggle, grasped together in the very attitude in which they had given the death-wounds. Here Lady Herbert, having lighted a lanthorn, began her hideous labour; turning over the stiff and heavy carcasses, touching the mangled limbs, and gazing on the ghastly distorted faces. Sometimes she shrank at discovering symptoms of half-extinguished life in bodies which appeared dead. Sometimes she heard groans, and half-muttered words which she could not interpret. Her hands and dress were stained with blood. Long did she thus persevere, but all in vain. Even her faithful servant had advised her to give up the search. Suddenly, as she kneeled beside a dead body, she felt a light cold touch on her hand, and, looking round, beheld a small dog. "Good heavens!" she exclaimed. "It is Fido! He may help us to find his master." "I'll warrant him so far forth," said Travers. "If it please your Ladyship to follow him, I'll lead the horses."

The animal (a beautiful small greyhound, which always attended Sir Edward) bounded forward, turning round from time to time with a sharp and cheerful bark, till he led them to a hillock, the sides of which were covered with slain. The dog forced his way between the bodies, and at last stopped where several were lying heaped on each other. He then pushed and tore with his snout and paws, looking round and whining and barking with great eagerness. Travers, leaving the horses, dragged off several bodies, and at last came to one which, from the tones and gestures of the animal, they could not doubt to be that of Sir Edward. He had been despoiled of his cloak, arms, and upper garments; but on bringing the lanthorn to his face they found that it was he. The body, covered with many wounds, was cold and stiff; and every feature seemed fixed in the stillness of death. The dog licked his face, scratched him with his paws, and used every effort to arouse him; and when all was in vain, sent forth a long and piteous howl. Lady Herbert and Travers raised the body, chafed the temples, applied strong scents to the nostrils; but without success. "Alas," said Travers, "'tis a lost labour. All we can do now is to procure a Christian burial." "Peace, Travers! Methinks I feel warmth about the heart. Let us bear him to yonder cottages. We may find help there."

They wrapped the body in the blanket which they had brought, and Travers, mounting his horse, supported it in his arms before him. Lady Herbert followed on foot, leading the other two horses. In this way they reached a small hamlet, the inmates of which had fled at the approach of the hostile armies. They entered the nearest cottage. No living creature was within; but the embers of a fire

remained unextinguished. These they carefully fed with wood till the flame revived.
They placed Sir Edward on a bed; applied
warmth to his body; rubbed him with strong
essences; and used all means to arrest and
restore the fleeting spirit. At length they
could perceive a change. The vital warmth
slowly extended from about the heart; a
feeble pulse was distinguishable, and gradually became firmer. Then he heaved a deep
sigh. It was the most grateful sound that ever
struck Lady Herbert's ear. Soon afterwards
he opened his languid eyes; gazed with a
bewildered look upon her, as she hung over
him; and, making an effort at recollection,
said, in a low and tremulous voice, " Mabel,
is it thou?"—"Yes, Edward: it is I: whom
else shouldst thou think to see at such an
hour?"

The wounds Sir Edward had received
were so severe, and his exhaustion from

cold and loss of blood was so great, that he was with difficulty removed from the cottage into the town of Northampton. There, however, it was dangerous to remain. The country around was all in possession of the Parliamentary forces; and the consequence of discovery would have been his immediate arrest. He was, therefore, secretly conveyed into Gloucestershire, to his own estate; but, as a residence at his own house would have led to detection, he was carried to a cottage at some distance, situated in a deep glen, and thickly surrounded by woods. Here, it was hoped, he might escape the parties of horse which, during the siege of Bristol, scoured the western country, and lived at free quarters on the inhabitants, as a penalty for their attachment to the Royal cause.

In this retirement he continued to gain strength. Lady Herbert, the better to lull

suspicion, appeared frequently with her family
at Northampton, and soon after ventured to
remove them to Oxford. From there she
often visited the cottage to watch over her
husband's recovery, making her journeys by
night attended by the faithful Travers. On
one of these occasions, as they approached
the cottage towards morning, they were
alarmed by perceiving strewed on the narrow
path which led into the glen fragments of
feathers, silk, and men's apparel. As they
came nearer, they saw the cottage door
standing open. Lady Herbert hastily dismounted, and, entering, found all within
empty and silent. The furniture, with some
musical instruments and papers, lay scattered
about and broken. Everything bore the
marks of disturbance and violence. "Good
heavens, Travers!" she cried. "What hath
befallen?"—"Alas, I fear me that the Roundheads have come down and surprised him;

but I will run to Gabriel's cottage and inquire. Will your Ladyship be pleased to tarry here till I return?" — " Nay, . Travers: methinks I had better go with thee."

They soon reached the old forester's dwelling, situated farther up the glen, where their fears were confirmed. " Alas, Lady," said the old man, "I think there be some false heart that hath betrayed him; or at least a shrewd mischance must have discovered his retreat to the rebels. For at yester eventide we saw troopers passing between the trees, and soon they fell into the path leading towards the cottage. My son Ned (mine honoured master's godson, so please your Ladyship) ran through the bushes to get before them and give the alarm; but he was too late. They had already seized upon the cottage, and Sir Edward was in their hands. When Ned ventured near, they let fly some bullets at him, and one took the tuft off his cap. As soon as they departed, we ran to the cottage, but found all gone." " Did you note which way they took ? " said Lady Herbert. "We were all on the watch, so please your Lady-ship, but durst not go near. However, to our thought they made toward Cirencester." " They must be for London," she said, "and thither will I follow."

Lady Herbert hastened towards London, taking on her way the town of Oxford, where she saw her children, and settled how they should be cared for in her absence. On her arrival in London, she found that Sir Edward had been committed to the Tower. Many were the intercessions used, and many the repulses suffered, before she could prevail with the fierce and fanatic rulers of that time to allow her to see her husband. She at length succeeded, through the influence of Mrs. Claypole, Cromwell's daughter. She found Sir Edward languishing under sickness and pain. His sudden journey, while scarcely recovered from his wounds, had brought on a relapse; and this had been little alleviated amid the neglect and hardships of a prison. His spirits were revived by the presence of his wife; but there was still room for cruel anxiety, both on his own account and for the Royal cause. Lady Herbert shared in these fears, but endeavoured to disguise them, and discharged the hard task of feigning hope which she could not feel. In the midst of these distresses, a day was fixed for Sir Edward's trial, the news of which affected his wife far more deeply than himself. She looked forward to the result, and expected neither justice nor mercy. The remembrance of Lord Strafford occurred to them both. Sir Edward burned to emulate his noble constancy; but Lady Herbert thought of his fate, and trembled.

The trial was conducted as such proceedings too often are in factious times when the accusers are judges and the accused are pre-condemned. Suffice it to say, that Sir Edward was charged with misleading the King by false counsels, and maintaining and abetting him in arms against his people. He was found guilty of treason, and sentenced to death.

The dreadful interval which ensued was employed by Lady Herbert in unavailing supplications for pardon. The charitable Mrs. Claypole again interfered, but without success. At length, rendered at once inventive and desperate by the approaching danger, Lady Herbert resolved upon a bold plan. She first despatched Travers to her family, with instructions to have them conveyed privately to France. He was directed to return immediately afterwards to the little seaport of Folkestone, and to engage a boat and remain there till joined by his master. · Then Lady Herbert, taking advantage of the permission to visit her husband, stated that she should not return home at night, and, exchanging clothes with him, dismissed him towards evening in her place. She then went to bed, on the pretext of illness, and thus remained unsuspected in place of Sir Edward till the next morning.

Sir Edward escaped to France. His wife's situation, however, was far from agree-able. The ruling faction, wroth at having the prey taken out of their grasp, wreaked their vengeance on the instrument of their disappointment. Her imprisonment was close and severe, varied only from time to time by a summons for examination before a Committee. When questioned as to her treasonable designs, "Alas, Sirs," said she,

" I had no design but to save my husband, and that was surely loyal. Which of you, on such enforcement, would have done less ? "

After some months' confinement, the Committee, feeling that the persecution of a noble and virtuous woman brought discredit on their cause, although they would not openly authorise her release, resolved to connive at her escape. She was, at the same time, given to understand that she must hasten her departure from England, as it would be necessary to make some show of pursuit, to satisfy their zealous adherents. Accordingly, she was permitted to leave the Tower, and proceeded on horseback towards the coast, with a single attendant. She took the road through Sussex keeping to the westward, as there she was less liable to discovery than she would have been in the nearer communications with France, and,

towards evening, reached the small fishing
town of Seaford, near Beachy Head. To
escape remark, her attendant stopped on the
outskirts of the town, and returned to
London with the horses by a different road.
Thus left alone, she knocked at the door of
a fisherman's cottage. The man opened it
himself, and she asked him if she could get
a boat to pass over to France. "A boat to
France!" he exclaimed. "Why, not to-
night, sure?"—"Yes, good friend: to-night,
if it be possible: my occasions brook no
delay."—"Why, there is nought but a light
wherry afloat, no bigger than a cockle shell.
You had better tarry till morning." Here
the fisherman's wife, overhearing a female
voice, came out with a child in her arms,
and several children hanging about her.
"It were a crazy thing," said she, "to go
afloat to-night: thou shalt do no such,
Jacob." "Peace, wench," cried he. "Sure,

I am old enough to answer for myself."
" Indeed, friends," said Lady Herbert, " I
am loth to trouble you. Yet it is very
needful I should go to-night, if you will
aid me so far. My strait is great, or I
would not ask you." This was spoken in
a voice and manner that gained upon these
rude but kindly people. " Jacob," said the
woman, "she seemeth a noble lady, and
many such are sore pressed in these times.
Thou must e'en do her will. But, lady,
wilt thou not consent to tarry all night in
our poor house? They will take thee
betimes in the morning."—" I pray thy
excuse, my good dame, though with thanks
for thy kindness. It is a heavy need which
urgeth me to be gone ; and, therefore, I do en-
treat both your furtherance." " Then, Jacob,"
said the woman, " thou must needs go. Hie
thee down to the Point, and get Will Roberts
to help thee."

While the fisherman was away, Lady Herbert remained with his wife, and completely won the poor woman's heart by her sweet and gracious manner towards herself and her children. This is a subject on which two mothers are never at a loss for conversation, however strangers to each other, or different in rank and circumstances. At length the man returned, and told them that all was ready. Lady Herbert, attended by the good woman and her children, went down to a little creek, where the boat was lying. Here another man stood waiting for them; and she took an affectionate leave of her humble companions, who in return put up prayers for her safety. Then she stepped on board. At this moment, a thought of her defenceless situation, embarking thus with two men strangers to her, and rude in their habits of life, came across her mind. She breathed a silent appeal to Heaven, and trusted to its protection. She read in the weather-beaten faces of her attendants signs of honest and simple hearts, and felt that she need not fear. Indeed, they regarded her with reverence as a superior being, and would have hazarded their lives in her protection.

The night was dark and squally; rain began to fall; and towards morning there came an adverse breeze, which raised the waves, tossing the little bark to and fro, and covering them with spray. The men pulled with all their vigour; but made little way; and as day broke, and the wind fell, they found themselves enveloped in a heavy mist, which prevented their seeing before them. At length, however, the mist cleared away, and they were relieved by a view of the French coast, which, after a tedious and stormy passage, they reached in safety, landing at the little port of Fecamp, in

Normandy. Here Lady Herbert took leave of her hardy conductors, with a liberal reward for their services, and set out to join her husband, in Paris.

To Sir Edward and her children the meeting was equally unexpected and gratifying; for during her imprisonment all correspondence had been forbidden, and they were full of apprehension about her at the time she appeared before them. Her joy at the reunion was cruelly damped by the appearance of her husband, whose pale and emaciated looks showed that his health had rather lost than gained since they were separated. Indeed, his anxiety at her situation, accompanied by a feeling of blame to himself as its cause, had kept his mind in a state of constant disquiet, and had aggravated his bodily ailment. Though his health improved a little on her arrival, the amendment was temporary; and it soon became evident that his life was ebbing away. His wife observed the fatal symptoms, but, amid her anguish, preserved an external composure. Every effort of skill and tenderness was tried in vain; and about four months after Lady Herbert had rejoined her husband, he died in her arms.

The trials of this noble woman had thitherto been of such a nature as called for active exertion. The lot which now became her portion was perhaps more difficult to bear: a long, unvarying course of exile, dependence, and neglect. Her husband's estates had been declared forfeited. Herself and her family were proscribed by the ruling powers. Her only resource was to retire to a small provincial town in France, where, by the assistance of her own and her husband's friends, whose fortunes had partly outlived the public storm, she procured a bare sufficiency for the wants of life. Such assistance was not discountenanced by Cromwell, whose faults were not those of a little mind. She devoted herself to the education of her children; constantly maintaining in herself, and instilling into them, resignation to the will of Providence, and a hope for better times.

Such times were long in coming, and for the first portion of her retreat sorrows seemed to accumulate around her. The tragic end of Charles I. filled her with grief and horror. Some time afterwards, when his son made an unsuccessful attempt to recover the Crown, Lady Herbert's eldest son, the inheritor of his father's accomplishments of mind and person, accompanied his Sovereign to England, and fell at the fatal field of Worcester, after performing deeds of skill and valour beyond his years. He died in the arms of the faithful Travers, who had attended him; and in his last moments sent a loving message to

his mother, and a ring which had belonged
to Sir Edward to his next brother. It bore
a head of Charles I., with the inscription,
"*Abyde Loyall.*"

At length Charles II. recovered the Throne
of his ancestors. Among those who offered
their congratulations on that event, Lady
Herbert sent Sir William, now her eldest son,
to pay his duty, and solicit the restoration of
his paternal estates. These still remained
sequestrated for public use, and had been
placed by Parliament at the King's disposal.
That voluptuous monarch, who was alike
devoid of gratitude and resentment, paid little
attention to the young man's claims, and
seemed more inclined to appropriate the
estates to his own pleasures, or to bestow
them on some of the profligate and greedy
favourites by whom he was surrounded. Sir
William wrote in a desponding strain to his
mother. "What?" said she. "Is it come

to this ? I must needs go myself, and lay before His Majesty all that we have done and suffered in his cause."

Lady Herbert, though advanced in years, retained much of the beauty of her early days; and the nobleness and dignity of her manners gained her the admiration and respect of the polite monarch and his gay and frivolous followers. Being admitted with two of her sons to his presence, she addressed him thus: "Your Majesty sees before you the widow of Edward Herbert, who perished by the wounds and hardships which he suffered in the service of Your Majesty's father. . You see the mother of another Edward Herbert, who died on the field of Worcester, fighting by Your Majesty's side; and a family who have endured long years of exile and poverty ; and by their loyalty have lost all, save honour ; who now seek but their own, which it is in Your Majesty's power to restore, and who (should it be given) will ever hold it as a trust to be freely employed in the same cause."

This address moved even the indifferent soul of Charles ; but its effect would soon have been effaced, amid the gaiety and laughter of his thoughtless companions, had not the better counsels of Clarendon and Ormonde prevailed, and saved the honour of their master. Through their influence, Lady Herbert's suit at length was granted. She soon found, however, that the Court of Charles was no place for her. It suited neither her habits nor her principles. Therefore, after gracefully returning her thanks to the King for his act of justice, she retired to her son's estate, and sought solace in the bosom of her family. Here, surrounded by domestic peace, in the remembrance of former scenes, and in exercises of piety and beneficence, Lady Herbert passed the remainder of her days, after a life chequered by many vicissitudes, darkened by many sorrows, but ennobled by the highest attributes of our nature—affection, courage, and patience.

THE END

Printed by R. & R. CLARK, LIMITED, *Edinburgh.*

In Square Crown 8vo. Printed on Light Paper, with Deckled Edges, and bound in Buckram. Price 6s.

A

PRISONER OF FRANCE

BEING

THE REMINISCENCES OF

THE LATE

CAPTAIN CHARLES BOOTHBY, R.E.

Containing a Frontispiece Portrait of the Author, and several small Illustrations from Pen-and-Ink Sketches in the Author's Journals.

This narrative begins with the Battle of Talavera, at which the chronicler, a young officer in the Royal Engineers, was disabled by a wound in the leg. It vividly describes the social conditions of France and Spain during the wars in the early part of the century, and in particular the chivalrous courtesy with which the French officers treated any enemies who fell into their hands.

A. & C. BLACK, SOHO SQUARE, LONDON, W.

In One Volume, Large Crown 8vo, Cloth, gilt top, price 7s. 6d.

THE HISTORY OF THE
REFORMATION OF RELIGION
WITHIN THE REALM OF SCOTLAND

WRITTEN BY

JOHN KNOX

EDITED FOR POPULAR USE BY

C. J. GUTHRIE, Q.C.

*WITH NOTES, SUMMARY, GLOSSARY, INDEX, AND
FIFTY-SIX ILLUSTRATIONS*

"The task is one which Carlyle desired to see accomplished nearly thirty years ago, when he wrote in one of the least known of his works: 'It is really a loss to English, and even to universal, literature, that Knox's hasty and strangely interesting, impressive, and peculiar book . . . has not been rendered far more extensively legible to serious mankind at large than is hitherto the case.' It will be interesting to see if Mr. Guthrie's labour can restore John Knox's 'History' to the place of honour it once held, but seems long to have lost, among Scottish classics."—*Glasgow Herald.*

A. & C. BLACK, SOHO SQUARE, LONDON, W.

ST. THOMAS OF CANTERBURY. A study of the evidence bearing on his Death and Miracles. By the Rev. EDWIN A. ABBOTT, D.D. In 2 Vols. Demy 8vo. Cloth. Containing Intaglio Plate Frontispiece. Price 24s.

Part I. gives translations of eleven Latin narratives of the Martyrdom, together with those of Garnier, and the Saga, comparing the whole with the modern accounts of Stanley and Tennyson, and deducing general rules of criticism applicable to synoptic documents. In Part II., the Miracles of St. Thomas are described from the books of Benedict and William of Canterbury, and those common to both writers are arranged in parallel columns, an attempt being made to show the authenticity of many of them, to trace their gradual degeneration, to indicate the origination and growth of legend, and to point out the bearing of the whole subject on the study of the Gospels.

THROUGH ARCTIC LAPLAND. By C. J. CUTCLIFFE HYNE. With a Map showing route, and containing 16 page Illustrations, also several small Pen-and-Ink Sketches by CECIL HAYTER, who accompanied the Author on his journey. Post 8vo. Cloth. Price 10s. 6d.

This work describes certain regions within the Arctic Circle which had not previously been explored by Europeans. It is less a record of sport and adventure than a chatty account of the curious ways and customs of Lapps, Finns, and other peoples of the Far North.

ROCK VILLAGES OF THE RIVIERA. By WILLIAM SCOTT. Containing over 50 Illustrations, mostly full-page, from pen-and-ink drawings by the Author. Square Crown 8vo. Cloth. Price 7s. 6d.

This book deals with some of those picturesque and out-of-the-way hamlets which visitors to the South may have seen perched on hill-tops or hidden in the valleys, away from the beaten track of tourists. The district referred to is that part of Liguria which commences at the French frontier ; and a brief historical outline traces the origin and development of these little "Ville"—as they were called—from the early days of the Genoese Republic, through the interesting period when some of them, revolting from the oppression of Ventimiglia, formed the "Community of the Otto Luoghi," and proceeded to carry out their ideas of Home Rule. Several of the villages still possess a number of their old documents, account-books, and other records, and these are now laid under contribution for the first time.

HISTORICAL INTRODUCTION TO THE PRIVATE LAW OF ROME. By the late Prof. J. MUIRHEAD, LL.D. New Edition. Revised and Edited by HENRY GOUDY, M.A., D.C.L., LL.D., Regius Professor of Civil Law, Oxford ; Fellow of All Souls College. Demy 8vo. Cloth. Price 21s.

THE MINISTER'S CONVERSION. A Novel. By I. HOOPER, Author of "His Grace o' the Gunne." Crown 8vo. Cloth. Price 6s.

A romantic study of the struggle between human nature and religious fervour in a dissenting community in the West of England. The novel is by the author of "His Grace o' the Gunne."

THE ENCHANTED STONE. A Novel. By C. LEWIS HIND. Crown 8vo. Cloth. Price 6s.

Founded on the theory, prevalent among Oriental peoples, that the ultimate Revelation will be in the West, the plot of this novel is laid in London amid the most modern conditions. The story, however, although exceedingly original and daring, is neither fantastic nor frivolous. On the contrary, it will commend itself not less to the philosophic student of religion than to the lover of an exciting tale.

A. & C. BLACK, SOHO SQUARE, LONDON, W.